GUNS FOR HIRE

Guns for Hire

Bradford Scott

WHEELER
CHIVERS

This Large Print edition is published by Wheeler Publishing, Waterville, Maine, USA and by AudioGO Ltd, Bath, England.
Wheeler Publishing, a part of Gale, Cengage Learning.

LIBRARY OF CONGRESS CATALOGING-IN-PUBLICATION DATA

Scott, Bradford, 1893–1975.
  Guns for hire / by Bradford Scott. — Large print ed.
    p. cm. — (Wheeler Publishing large print western)
  ISBN-13: 978-1-4104-3980-2 (softcover)
  ISBN-10: 1-4104-3980-1 (softcover)
  1. Large type books. I. Title.
PS3537.C9265G86 2011
813'.54—dc22   2011017530

BRITISH LIBRARY CATALOGUING-IN-PUBLICATION DATA AVAILABLE

Published in 2011 in the U.S. by arrangement with Golden West Literary Agency.
Published in 2012 in the U.K. by arrangement with Golden West Literary Agency.

U.K. Hardcover: 978 1 445 83846 5 (Chivers Large Print)
U.K. Softcover: 978 1 445 83847 2 (Camden Large Print)

Printed in the United States of America
1 2 3 4 5 6 7 15 14 13 12 11

GUNS FOR HIRE

1

Lounging easily in the saddle, Ranger Walt Slade, named by the Mexican *peons* of the Rio Grande river villages, *El Halcón* — The Hawk — gazed at the advancing sparkle of lights that were as earthbound reflections of the blazing Texas stars above.

There were two clusters of lights, one larger than the other, with a broad band of blackness between.

Slade's gaze was appreciative, for after many miles of the lonely sage-covered hills of the Zapata-Roma region and the barren, semi-arid plains of the Laredo section, anything hinting at human occupancy and companionship was cheering. The larger cluster of lights marked Laredo, the small was Nuevo Laredo across the river in Mexico. The band of blackness was the turgid flood of the Rio Grande.

"Well, Shadow," he remarked to his magnificent black horse, "looks like we'll get a chance to put on the nosebag before long, and we can both stand a good surrounding. Sort of lean rations of late. So june along, horse, not too much farther to go. We should make it without any trouble."

El Halcón was unduly optimistic.

Really there were just about three miles more to cover, but after a long and hard day beginning before sunup, that was enough. So despite the pangs of hunger gnawing at his vitals, Slade let the tired horse choose his own gait.

Soon he sighted more lights, on his left and close to the river bank, wide-spaced. Low-lying, lonely, and discouraged looking lights, little beads of feeble fire striving to push back the crowding darkness. They marked, he knew, the start of the great irrigation project that would eventually change the semi-arid land into a garden spot, though not without difficulty and strife.

The project that, incidentally, Slade had been instrumental in getting under way nearly a year before. He pulled to a halt and for some moments sat contemplating them.

"Progress, horse," he remarked to Shadow. "That will in the end mean prosperity and comfort for many. But there are always those who try to stop the wheels, for one reason or another. They can't stop them, but by shovelling sand into the gears they may slow them a bit. Why in this instance? I don't know, yet, but I intend to find out. That's why we're back here again, horse — to try and root out the shovelers. Haven't the least idea who they are, but it's up to us to find out."

He raised his eyes and glanced toward Laredo's shadowy waterfront, which always interested him. Plenty of stirring happenings down there, some of which he had personally experienced during his former visit to the river town. He was about to gather up the reins and move on when abruptly he stiffened in the saddle, staring.

From the dark and murky band which was the river had erupted a dazzling glare that flickered Laredo's lights and seemed to dim the very stars above.

The blinding flash vanished, the dark rushed down, but instantly followed a rising glow. To Slade's ears drifted a deep and sullen rumble.

With appalling swiftness the glow spread and strengthened. Buildings stood out in stark relief. Revealed was a big river steamer, its deck a seething mass of flame.

"What in blazes!" the Ranger exclaimed aloud. "Sounded like an oil or gasoline drum let go. Wasn't dynamite; the explosion wasn't sharp enough for that. Get going, horse, this will stand a mite of looking into."

Shadow, sensing an emergency, stepped out briskly, swiftly quickening his pace. Slade leaned forward in the saddle, his eyes fixed on the distant fire. At times the flames would dull a trifle, as if water were being poured on them, then roar up more fiercely than before.

They covered a fast mile and more. Now the trail was crooked as a snake in a cactus patch and flanked by a straggle of brush that at times obscured the fire.

Suddenly a sound reached Slade's keen ears, a sound he quickly recognized as fast hoofs drumming the hard surface of the trail, coming from the direction of town. He pulled over against the brush to the right and drew rein. Not good judgment to barge head-on into a bunch of riders on this trail, especially at night.

Around the bend, only a few yards distant, bulged five horsemen going like the wind. There was a yelp of alarm. Slade hurled himself sideways from the saddle even as a gun blazed, the slug whining through the space his body had occupied an instant before.

Prone on the ground, he drew and shot

with both hands as the riders swept past. A yell of pain echoed the boom of the big Colts and in the starshine he saw an arm fly up wildly. A second man lurched forward in the saddle, grabbing the horn for support. Then the band flashed around the next bend, Slade speeding them on their way with wrathful bullets. Holding his fire, he listened intently; the beat of hoofs continued, fading into the distance. He got to his feet, dusted himself off and said several things that wouldn't look nice in print.

"Now what the devil was that all about?" he wondered angrily aloud. "Nice friendly reception committee. Welcome to Laredo! I've a notion those hellions may have had something to do with that fire. Something sure had them sifting sand, and with guilty consciences I'd say, the way they threw down on me, for no reason at all. Well, I figure a couple of them have something to remember me by. Okay, horse, let's try it again."

Still muttering angrily, he swung into the saddle and headed for Laredo. Clearing the brush, he saw that the fire was still burning but not so fiercely as before. Looked like they were getting the darn thing under control. Appeared the steamer would need a considerable chore of repairs, though.

Watchful and alert, he continued on his way without further incident and a little later he was riding south on Bernardo Avenue, which led to the waterfront where the Rio Grande, after flowing due south past the town, made a sharp bend to the east. The burning steamer was but a couple of blocks east of the International Bridge at the foot of Convent Avenue.

Laredo had a fire department of sorts, and when Slade drew rein at the outskirts of a crowd watching the fire, a couple of pumpers were pouring water onto the steamer's deck, which was now but little more than a charred ruin. Slade quickly noted that other firemen were shovelling salt and sand onto the smolders; it was a gasoline or oil fire, all right.

Dismounting, he dropped the split reins to the ground, all that was necessary to keep Shadow right where he was, and sauntered forward, deftly easing his way through the throng to the front, pausing beside a jolly looking Mexican in police uniform. Laredo's police force being composed, in equal numbers of Texans and Mexicans.

"How did it start, *amigo?*" he asked in flawless Spanish.

The short policeman glanced up at the sternly handsome face so far above his own,

12

smiled, and voiced a Spanish greeting. But when he answered Slade's question, he spoke colloquial English, as Mexican Texans of several generations usually did.

"She was carrying oil drums on her deck and I reckon one of 'em blew up," he said. "Sprayed fire all over everything. That old greasy, worm-eaten deck blazed up like a torch. If it hadn't been for a lucky thing I reckon she would have burned to the water."

"How's that?" Slade asked.

"The fire boys were just coming back from a little blaze over on Zaragoza Street, had their horses hitched up and everything," the policeman explained. "So they got here and went to work in a couple of minutes and had everything under control mighty fast."

"I see," Slade nodded. "That was a lucky break. Wonder why there was only one explosion, though? Looks like the heat would have generated explosive gas in those drums."

"Never thought of that, but you're right," the policeman acknowledged. "Was funny."

"Do you happen to know what other cargo she is packing?" Slade asked.

"Tools and materials for the irrigation works, I think," the policeman replied.

Slade nodded again, his eyes thoughtful.

Now the fire was pretty well beaten out,

the crowd of onlookers thinning. Slade speculated the scorched vessel for a moment.

"She'll just about need a new deck, but I've a notion her cargo is intact," he observed. "Looks like things are under control, so I guess I'd better stable my horse; time he puts on the nosebag. Hope I'll see you again."

"I expect you will," the policeman replied cheerfully. He twinkled his eyes at the Ranger, lowered his voice.

"Sheriff Medford will be glad to see you, and so will — others," he said. Slade shot him a glance.

"You know me, eh?"

The policeman smiled, and broke into flowery Spanish.

"*Si,* I know you, *Capitan.* Who does not know *El Halcón,* the just, the good, the compassionate, the friend of the lowly. *Capitan,* I am honored!"

"*Gracias, amigo,*" Slade said, his cold eyes suddenly all kindness. "*Gracias!*"

"*Vaya usted con Dios!*" the policeman murmured.

"Thank you again," Slade said. "*Hasta luego!*" With a smile and a nod, he turned and strode to his patiently waiting horse. The little policeman followed him with an

14

admiring gaze.

What a splendid-looking man he was, the policeman thought. And he was right. Walt Slade was tall, more than six feet, with shoulders and a chest slimming down to a lean, sinewy waist that matched his height.

The face that was in accord to his magnificent height was arresting. A rather wide mouth, grin-quirked at the corners, relieved somewhat the tinge of fierceness evinced by the prominent hawk nose above and the powerful jaw and chin beneath. A pushed-back broad-brimmed and somewhat battered "J.B." revealed a broad forehead and thick, crisp black hair.

The striking countenance was dominated by long, black-lashed eyes of very pale gray. Cold, reckless eyes that nevertheless most always seemed to have gay little devils of laughter lurking in their clear depths. Devils, however, that, did occasion warrant, would leap to the front and be anything but laughing.

El Halcón wore the careless, efficient garb of the rangeland — bibless overalls known as "Levi's" and favored by cowhands, soft blue shirt with vivid neckerchief looped at the throat, and well scuffed half-boots of softly tanned leather — and he wore it with debonair grace.

Around his waist were double cartridge belts, from the carefully worked and oiled holsters of which protruded the plain black butts of heavy guns. And from those gun-handles, flaring out from his lean hips, his slender, muscular hands seemed never far away.

His horse was fitting to its master, fully eighteen hands high, his glossy coat and rippling mane of midnight black, his lines denoting both speed and endurance.

A gallant man on a gallant horse — the picture was complete. So thought the little policeman, as others before him had thought.

2

Riding north on Bernardo Avenue, Slade headed for Montezuma Street, where he knew there was a small hotel favored by cattlemen with nearby a reliable livery stable that would accommodate Shadow. He stopped at the stable first.

The stable keeper remembered both man and horse and voiced a warm greeting. Confident that the big black would lack for nothing, Slade shouldered his saddle pouches and repaired to the hotel, where he had no difficulty acquiring a room in which he deposited the pouches.

His next stop was a saloon that had been named for the street or the street for the saloon, he never learned which. Anyhow, it had "Montezuma" legended across a broad expanse of plate glass.

He doubted if the ancient Aztec emperor would have been flattered had he risen from the grave and poked his classic nose into the place. For the Montezuma was turbulent and rowdy. However, it put out an excellent surrounding of tasty chuck and Sheriff Tobe Medford had recommended it highly on the occasion of Slade's former visit to Laredo.

Incidentally, it was decidedly more ornate than the average cattle-country saloon. The mirror-blazing back bar was pyramided with bottles of every shape and color. The short-skirted, low-cut dresses of the dance floor girls were of excellent material. The long bar which claimed a resemblance to mahogany was highly polished, and the stacked dishes on the lunch counter were spotless and shining. The roulette wheels were decorated and bright. The Mexican orchestra was in costume. And the bartenders actually wore white coats.

So far as Slade could see, the Montezuma hadn't changed a bit in nearly a year. The same noisy and cheerful crowd lined the bar, occupied the gaming tables and thumped boots on the dance floor, and it was typical Border cow country. There were overalled punchers, Mexicans in black velvet ornamented with much silver, conservatively dressed townspeople. And more than one or two gentlemen who, Slade shrewdly suspected, very likely preferred to do most of their riding between the hours of sunset and sunrise.

Of course there were new faces, but the general atmosphere was the same.

Locating a vacant table near the dance floor, Slade sat down and ordered a meal. John Gorty, the owner, spotted him at once and came hurrying across the room with outstretched hand.

"Mr. Slade!" he exclaimed. "Say, it's good to see you again. Was getting scairt maybe you'd forgotten us."

"Couldn't possibly do so," Slade replied smilingly as they shook hands. "I have some pleasant memories of the Montezuma, and elsewhere. Take a load off your feet, John."

"Uh-huh, *elsewhere,* that I can understand," chuckled Gorty as he occupied a chair. He summoned the waiter with a preemptory wave of his plump hand.

"Only the best," he ordered, "and fetch my private bottle from under the bar. This calls for a mite of celebration.

"I'm expecting Tobe Medford any minute," he added as the waiter filled glasses to the brim. "He ain't had his evening helpin' yet — guess the fire down on the riverfront held him up."

"Wouldn't be surprised," Slade conceded. "I'll be glad to see him." He hoped to get a lowdown on the fire from the sheriff; he had already formed his own opinion relative to the conflagration.

A few minutes later, the waiter arrived with Slade's dinner and the Ranger set to it with the appreciation of a man who had found good food scarce of late. Gorty motioned to the waiter to refill the glasses.

"See you after a bit," he said and ambled back to the far end of the bar to attend to his many chores.

Finally, with his meal consumed, Slade leaned back in his chair with a cup of fragrant steaming coffee and rolled a cigarette. He was smoking in full-fed content when Sheriff Tobe Medford entered, glanced around, stared and strode to the table.

"Well, I'll be hanged!" he exclaimed.

"Hope so," Slade agreed cheerfully. "How are you, Tobe?"

"Might have known it! Might have known it!" snorted the sheriff as he shook hands and slumped into a chair. "You and trouble always manage to show up together. Been hoping you'd amble in soon. Things are a mess."

"So I gathered from your letter to Captain McNelty," Slade said. "He figured I'd better drop in for a look-see."

"Suppose you saw the fire," Medford

remarked, after he had given the waiter his order.

"Yes, I saw it," Slade admitted. "I was out on the trail when it started. They had it under control by the time I reached the riverfront."

"What do you think of it?"

Slade shrugged his broad shoulders. "Plain sabotage, in line with similar incidents I understand have been happening hereabouts of late."

"What makes you think so?" the sheriff asked curiously.

"Well," Slade replied, "It is reasonable to assume those oil drums stacked on the steamer's deck were empty. Otherwise you would have had one explosion after another that would probably have blown the whole waterfront to smithereens."

"Guess you're right about that, per usual," the sheriff admitted. "I never thought of it, and I doubt if anybody else did, either. But what does it mean?"

Slade countered with a question of his own.

"She loaded at Brownsville?"

"That's right," nodded the sheriff.

"And," Slade said, "a drum of gasoline was slipped in with the empty oil drums and triggered somehow to catch fire and

21

explode. Just how I'm not prepared to say, at the moment."

Sheriff Medford shook his head in admiration. "Never miss a bet, do you?"

"Doesn't pay to miss too many," Slade smiled reply. "I very nearly missed one out on the trail this evening."

"How's that?" the sheriff asked.

Slade regaled him with an account of his gun fight with the mysterious riders.

"Where I made my mistake was in not sliding into the brush out of sight," he concluded. "It came close to being a fatal one."

"It would have been fatal for anybody who don't think and act like you do, and I never met anybody else who did," Medford growled. "Do you figure those hellions had something to do with the fire?"

"I don't know, but it would seem logical to presume they did," Slade replied. "For some reason or other, they appeared mighty anxious to get away from town as quickly as possible. Anything else off-color happen here tonight?"

The sheriff shook his head. "Not that I've heard about," he admitted. "And if anything did, I most likely would have heard before now." Slade nodded agreement.

However, something else off-color *had*

22

happened, which the sheriff would hear about before long.

While Medford addressed himself to his food, Slade sat silent, smoking thoughtfully. When the sheriff pushed back his empty plate with a satisfied sigh, hauling out his pipe and stuffing it with tobacco, he observed:

"I gather from your letter that somebody is deliberately endeavoring to slow up or discourage the irrigation project. Any notion who, or why?"

"No, I haven't," Medford replied. "Of course you know the cowmen don't favor it over-much. They figure it'll bring in more and more farmers, and all sorts of undesirable characters along with them. But that ain't all. Fact is, some of them are quite a bit worried. You see, quite a few of the boys' titles are a mite shaky, based on old Spanish and Mexican grants as they are, and there's a yarn going around that the irrigation people plan to eventually take over the whole section. Sounds loco, I know, but there are folks who believe it. And they wouldn't want to go up against a court fight to prove their titles are sound. Remember the crooked Land Committee you busted up here last year? Those hellions were preying on the little fellers, with forged documents and such and scarin' 'em into selling their holdings to the Committee for practically nothing. Or even resorting to murder like what happened to Sebastian Telo — shoved off a cliff."

Slade nodded, and his eyes were colder than their wont.

"But now," the sheriff resumed, "it's the big fellers who are bothered. All of a sudden they find themselves in the same corral the little fellers were, or so they think. This time *they* are the ones who have to do some scratching around to find evidence to bolster the authenticity of their grants or the grants of the fellers they or their dads bought the land from. Maybe they figure if they hold up the project enough, the folks over East who are putting in the money will pull out and the whole project will fall through.

"That's one angle. Then, too, the gents who hang out in the hills and the brush country, don't like the notion, knowing darn well it will eventually bring real law and order to the section. And of course you know the conditions in the Zapata-Roma section over to the east of here."

"Yes, the holdings there, many of them, at least, date back to the original grant given Tomas Sanchez by Don Jose de Escandon, colonizer of the region for the Spanish king.

24

Fifteen *sitios de ganado mayor* — the old grant read. Fifteen square leagues of range land. In return, Sanchez agreed to found a settlement at his own expense and to maintain a ferry 'for the convenience of traffic and the royal service.' He named the settlement Laredo in honor of his patron's home town in Spain.

"Sanchez was shrewd, and he knew cattle land and chose only the best, a good portion of which he deeded over to his followers, whose descendants own the land to this day."

"Looks like they hold title, all right," commented Medford.

"Yes," Slade agreed, "it looks that way. But after Mexico gained independence from Spain, the Mexican Government voided the grant. However, before any action could be taken, the Texas-Mexico War cut loose, Texas won independence from Mexico and the Mexican decree had no force. But it did cast a shadow of doubt over the validity of those titles. Those holdings became an independent civil settlement of Spanish ranchers that spread northward across the Rio Grande, and as such they still are. The owners now, of course, are Texans of Spanish descent. Just what would happen did the matter ever come to a court fight, I'm

25

not prepared to say, but it is not illogical that those owners are somewhat apprehensive and attach some significance to the rumor that the irrigation project aims to try and gain title. For which you can't blame them. Down around Brownsville was a somewhat similar condition and trouble and bloodshed came out of it.

"Incidentally, those folks aren't the kind you can push around with impunity, and very serious trouble could arise did they really believe for sure the irrigation people have anything of the sort in mind. See how the situation stands?"

"Yes, blast it! It's a mess!" growled the sheriff. "And what the devil are we going to do about it?"

"I don't know for sure, yet," Slade admitted. "I'll have to look things over before venturing an opinion as to what is to be done. But what happened tonight is a sample of what could be in store for Laredo and the whole section between here and Roma if something isn't done. Well, we'll see. How about a snort?"

"I need a dozen," Medford rumbled, hammering the table for service. "By the way, do you suppose those hellions who threw lead at you tonight recognized you as *El Halcón?*"

"Not impossible, but I rather doubt it," Slade replied. "The light wasn't overly good and I think it more likely that they just saw a figure looming up in front of them all of a sudden, and a guilty conscience makes for a nervous trigger finger. That is, assuming that they had something to do with the fire."

"There are plenty of sidewinders here-abouts that ain't got any use for *El Halcón,* after what you handed to more than a few of their brand when you were here last year," said Medford. "Reckon they're still trying to figure just what you got out of it, with your reputation for horning in on the good things other folks have started and skimmin' off the cream.

"That blasted *El Halcón* foolishness is going to get you into trouble sooner or later," he added querulously. "Some fool peace officer is liable to throw down on you some time, to say nothing of some gun slinger out to get a reputation by downing the notorious *El Halcón,* the singingest man in the whole Southwest with the fastest gunhand, as folks say about you, and not above shooting in the back to get it."

Which was exactly what Captain Jim Mc-Nelty, the famous Commander of the Border Battalion of the Texas Rangers, more than once declared, fearful that his Lieutenant and aceman would come to harm.

Due to his habit of working under cover whenever possible and often not revealing his Ranger connections, Walt Slade had built up a singular dual reputation. Those who knew the truth were wont to declare that he was the ablest as well as the most fearless of the Rangers. Others, who knew him only as *El Halcón,* a blasted owlhoot too smart to get caught, so far, maintained just as vigorously that he *was* just a confounded outlaw who'd get his comeuppance sooner or later.

Still others, who also knew him only us *El Halcón,* emphatically defended his deeds. "Got killings to his credit, eh?" they would reply to his detractors. "Ever hear of him killing anybody who didn't have one long overdue?"

"That's beside the point. A private citizen's got no business taking the law into his own hands. That's for the duly elected or appointed peace officers."

"Uh-huh, but when your duly elected or appointed peace officers can't handle the chore, *El Halcón* steps in, and *he* handles it."

So the discussion raged, and Slade paid them little mind and went his carefree way as *El Halcón,* knowing that by doing so, he opened up avenues of valuable information that would be denied a known Ranger, and that outlaws, thinking they had but one of their own brand to deal with, sometimes grew a mite careless, to their grief.

"Well," began the sheriff, "I think I'll — what the devil?"

A man had just rushed in, gasping as if he had run fast and far. He glared wildly about, spied the sheriff and fairly galloped to the table.

"The Albemarle Company!" he panted. "The Albemarle Company!"

3

"What in blazes is the matter with you?" bawled the sheriff. "What about the Albemarle Company? Cool down, will you, and tell us what the devil are you talking about?"

Thus adjured, the man grew slightly calmer and caught his breath, although he was still a trifle incoherent.

"They killed the watchman, busted open the safe and cleaned it . . . ten thousand dollars and more, somebody said."

"Who was it?" demanded Medford.

"Don't nobody know," replied the informant. "Didn't know nothin' till a feller stumbled over the watchman lyin' by the door with his head split open. Figured you should know about it. I ran all the way."

"You sound like you did," growled the sheriff, shoving aside his empty glass.

Walt Slade stood up. "Come on," he said, "let's go see what really happened."

Accompanied by the still gabbling messenger, they hurried from the saloon, a crowd that had overheard the conversation streaming after them.

Upon reaching the Albemarle Company offices and warehouse, which was close to where the still smoldering steamer had been secured to the dock, Slade's first thought was for the watchman, who lay on his face near a half-open door, his hair matted with blood. He knelt beside the body, turned it over gently, glanced at the man's lips, placed a hand over his heart.

"Isn't dead," he said quietly. With sensitive fingertips he probed the vicinity of an ugly gash above and slightly to the rear of the left temple.

"No indications of fracture, so far as I can ascertain, but there could be concussion; he got a nasty lick. Doc Beard still in town?"

"That's right," replied the sheriff.

"Send somebody to fetch him," Slade directed. "This fellow needs expert attention."

The sheriff did so. The crowd was grouped around the door, but nobody had ventured to enter.

"Come on, Tobe, let's see what's inside. Tell folks to stay out . . . don't want them tramping on something that might be of value as evidence. There's a bracket lamp

31

just inside the door. Get it."

Holding the lamp high, they entered the office. The light showed a big iron safe against one wall. The door stood partly open. The combination knob had been neatly drilled out and lay on the floor.

"Whoever did it knew his business," Slade remarked. "We'll take a look inside the safe and see if we can find anything of interest."

They approached the rifled strongbox. The sheriff reached out a hand to widen the door opening.

"Look out!" Slade roared. "Don't touch it." His amazingly keen eyes had noted what the sheriff didn't see. A thin, thread-like wire stretched from the damaged door to the interior of the safe.

Medford jerked his hand back as from a snake. "What the devil?" he sputtered.

"I don't know," Slade replied, "but it doesn't look good. Give me the lamp."

He held it close to the half-open door, peered inside, and gave a low whistle.

"Get everybody away from the building," he ordered. "Carry the watchman's body farther away . . . handle him carefully."

When *El Halcón* spoke in that tone of voice, the sheriff knew better than to argue or ask questions. He proceeded to do as he was told. Slade held the lamp still closer and shook his head.

As the sheriff was shoving the crowd back, a man dodged past him and hurried into the office, his eyes fixed on the safe.

"Get out of here," Slade told him.

"Listen," the other said, "I'm the cashier of —"

"Get out before I throw you out!" Slade blared at him and took a step forward. The cashier got out, hurriedly. A moment later the sheriff called from the door, "All set . . . everybody in the clear."

"You get with them," Slade said, turning back to the safe.

"You go to hell!" growled the sheriff and strode forward until he was but a pace behind the Ranger. Slade grinned at him over his shoulder.

"Okay," he capitulated. "If things don't work out right, we'll have company on a long, long trip. Take a look."

Medford leaned close and peered into the safe, and swore, his eyes widening.

Jammed into one of the rifled compartments was a cocked gun. The wire from the safe door was secured to the trigger. Its muzzle was trained on a neat bundle of six sticks of dynamite.

"Nice little contraption, eh?" Slade observed. "Enough powder there to blow the whole building into the bay, which is just what would have happened did anyone touch the door."

The sheriff gulped in his throat. "And I was reaching for the infernal thing," he said.

"You didn't quite make it and that's all that counts," Slade said cheerfully. "Now let's see if I can dismantle that thing without blowing us both to smithereens. That hogleg is set at a bad angle to handle, but I believe I can do it. You hold the lamp."

The sheriff held his breath as well as the lamp as *El Halcón* reached a cautious hand into the safe. Working with the utmost care, he finally managed to hook a thumb over the cocked hammer, a finger around the trigger. His hold on the very tip of the hammer wasn't any too good, but it was the best he could do. He put forth a gentle pressure on the trigger; the wire looped around it made that difficult also.

Slowly, gradually the trigger came back. Slade's thumb tightened on the hammer, felt the milled tip slip a trifle, and held *his* breath. The muscles of his wrist swelled as he eased the hammer forward.

A little more, and a little more; his thumb slipped again! Then, after what seemed an eternity of agonizing effort, the hammer was all the way down.

"All safe now," he said cheerfully, withdrawing his hand. The sheriff exhaled his breath with a whoosh, and mopped his brow. Slade chuckled. Then abruptly his eyes grew thoughtful.

"Come to think of it, the Albemarle Company is the servicing company for the irrigation project. Right?"

"That's right," agreed the sheriff, still mopping. "That steamer that was set afire is one of their boats." Slade nodded.

"Call the cashier in," he directed. "Keep everybody else out."

Medford went to the door and shouted, "Bob!" A moment later the cashier reappeared, glancing apprehensively at Slade, who beckoned him to the safe. The cashier stared, and looked dazed. Slade spoke.

"Very likely whoever rigged that infernal machine figured that a high official of the Albemarle Company would be the first to approach the safe," he remarked casually.

The cashier continued to stare into the safe. His face whitened and he began to sweat. Sheriff Medford repressed a grin.

"Walt," he said, "this is Bob Olney, vice-president and cashier for the Albemarle Company. Bob, this is Walt Slade, an *amigo* of mine, and he's been a mighty good friend to *you* tonight."

Olney reached out a hand that trembled a little. "Mr. Slade,' he said thickly, "I guess all I can say is thank you. But if *you* ever feel the need of a friend, no matter for what, don't hesitate to call on Bob Olney."

"Thank you, Mr. Olney," Slade smiled as they shook, the cashier's clasp warm and firm despite the agitation that still gripped him.

"Walt, do you figure it was that bunch you met on the trail?" Medford asked.

"I lean definitely to that opinion, now," Slade replied. "I sure wish I had gotten a look at their faces, but the light was very poor. I'd say from the way they backed their horses, that they were or had been range riders.

"It was a carefully planned and smoothly executed scheme," he continued. "Everybody, of course, including the watchman, had eyes only for the fire. So they belted the watchman one, took his keys and entered the office, doubtless locking the door behind them. With little fear of interruption, they took their time and did a slick job. Had everything worked out as they planned, I've a notion it would have given the irrigation folks quite a jolt."

"It sure would have," Olney declared emphatically. "They're jumpy enough as is."

Slade nodded.

"The robbery, of course, is common knowledge," he added thoughtfully, "but I've a notion it would be wise for we three to keep this particular angle here under our hats."

His hearers nodded their understanding.

Turning back to the safe, Slade ripped the gun free and passed it to the sheriff. The bundle of dynamite followed. Medford shoved the iron under his belt and carefully stowed the dynamite in a capacious coat pocket.

"Hope nobody whacks me before I get this stuff stowed in my office safe," he observed.

While Olney examined the rifled safe, Slade searched the room for a possible clue to the identity of the robbers, and failed to find one.

"They cleaned her, all right, to the last peso," Olney announced.

"How much did they get, Bob?" the sheriff asked.

"A few hundred more than ten thousand," Olney replied. "The money is covered by insurance, but when I think of what would have happened if it wasn't for Mr. Slade, I get the shakes all over again."

With a final glance around, Slade led the

way from the office. Outside they found Doc Beard had already arrived and under his ministrations the watchman had recovered consciousness. However, he had nothing to add to what Slade had already surmised.

"I was standing by the door watching the fire when all of a sudden the sky fell in on me," he said. "That's all I remember till I woke up with a devil of a headache and found Doc working on me."

"If you didn't have a skull like a cannon ball I wouldn't have had anything to do," Doc growled. "As it is, go and get drunk; will be the best thing for you. How are you, Walt? Reckon business is due to pick up for me. Always does when you show up."

Olney headed for home. The watchman, his duties over for the night, at Olney's direction, shambled off with sympathetic companions. The crowd quickly dissipated.

"And now," suggested the sheriff, "suppose we amble over to Miguel Sandoval's cantina for a snort and some coffee. Be quieter there than at the Montezuma and we'll be less pestered by jabberers asking darn fool questions. Folks at Miguel's place are discreet and don't ask questions."

"That's where Marie Telo used to work before we managed to get back the ranch the Land Committee stole from her and Rosa, her sister, and Rosa's husband, Estaban," Slade remarked.

The sheriff's mustache twitched slightly in a suppressed grin.

"That's right," he said.

"How are the Telos?" Slade asked casually. "I must ride over to their place soon." The sheriff's mustache twitched again.

"They're doing fine," he replied. "Fact is, they're mighty well heeled now. The irrigation folks offered them a big price for their river bottom acres. Estaban is a born cattleman and isn't interested in farming . . . his cows keep him busy. So they accepted. Little Marie is a rich woman, now."

"Fine!" Slade applauded. "She's a good girl and deserves a break.

"Is she married now?" he asked, even more casually.

For the third time the sheriff's mustache twitched. Which Slade, occupied by his own thoughts, failed to notice.

"Not that I've heard tell of," Medford replied to his question. "Wouldn't be surprised if she's received plenty of offers. She's a mighty purty gal, and all that dinero ain't be to be sneezed at."

"Guess you're right on both counts,"

Slade conceded, a trifle morosely. And for the fourth time the mustache twitched.

4

Miguel's cantina proved to be just as it was when Slade last visited it — softly lighted, spotlessly clean, with the excellent orchestra playing dreamy music. The dance floor girls were young and pretty.

Suddenly he halted, staring. Standing beside the orchestra platform was a girl wearing a low-cut bodice and the spangled short skirt of a dance floor girl. She was a slender, graceful little thing with great sloe eyes, a creamily tanned complexion and sweetly formed lips that were the scarlet of the hibiscus bloom. Even as he stared, she turned and glanced in his direction.

The big eyes widened. She uttered a glad little cry, raced across the room and fairly flung herself into his arms.

"So you *did* come back!" she exclaimed.

"Looks sorta that way," he conceded, holding her close. "I told you I would."

"But I didn't believe you," she said reproachfully. "And you haven't changed a bit."

"You have," he countered. "You're even more beautiful than you formerly were. But what in blazes are you doing here? Why aren't you out on the ranch? And the sheriff tells me you're a rich woman now and don't need to work."

Miss Marie Telo strugged daintily as she slipped from his arms and led him and the sheriff to a nearby table.

"Uh-huh, that's what *I* thought," she replied. "Only it didn't pan out that way. Didn't take me long to become bored to tears, with nothing to do, and realize I had to work if I wanted to be content. Estaban takes care of everything on the ranch, and Rosa takes care of Estaban. I was just a fifth wheel on the wagon. So I came back to Miguel.

"I'm sort of a privileged character here," she added, with a giggle. "I take care of all his book work and the stock, and so forth. I only go on the floor when I'm of a mind to. Which is frequently, I'll admit. As you know, I love to dance, and it's always gay and interesting out here.

"Besides," she added demurely, "I knew that if you *did* come back you'd be here shortly." She turned to the sheriff.

42

"Uncle Tobe, I'll wager you brought him here tonight," she said.

"Well, I did sorta suggest it," the sheriff admitted, with a chuckle.

"And he didn't tell me you were here," Slade said indignantly.

"Wanted to surprise you," said Medford.

"Well, you sure did, and most pleasantly," Slade declared. "How does it feel to be rich, Marie?"

"Oh, there are certain advantages in not having to watch my pennies," she replied. "I have my own nice little place here in town, with a garden and flowers and everything."

"Everything?"

She smiled and dimpled. "Well, not *everything*," she admitted, her eyes dancing.

"Or I didn't have," she added softly.

They laughed together. The sheriff chuckled.

"Darned if I don't believe I can eat something," he announced. Marie beckoned a waiter. "How about you, Walt?" she asked.

"The sheriff sets a good example," *El Halcón* agreed.

"And now suppose you tell me about all the wonderful and terrible things you've been getting into during the past year," Marie said. "Not your various conquests; I don't want to hear about *them!* Oh, I know,

43

my dear, you are irresistible to women, and to you, women are — irresistible. Just tell us the nice things, like being shot at."

"Like the time you carved a couple of notches on your gun stock?" he observed pointedly.

Marie shuddered. "Don't remind me of it," she begged. "I had to shoot that time. Those awful men were going to murder you."

"And if it hadn't been for you, they would have succeeded in doing just that," Slade declared.

"Yep, she sure saved your bacon for you," the sheriff chimed in.

Marie deftly changed the subject. "Please, Walt, tell us what you have been doing since you were here last," she said.

Thus importuned, Slade began to talk. Very quickly, however, Marie sighed and shook her head.

"It's no use," she told the sheriff. "There's no getting the truth from him. He just makes it sound like he got all the breaks and was just lucky. I give up!"

"Plenty of folks will tell you that Slade will talk, but he won't tell you anything," said Medford, shaking his head at the Ranger with mock disapproval.

Their orders arrived and were consumed

with relish. Miguel, the owner, came over and greeted Slade warmly and insisted they have a drink from his private bottle. After which Medford glanced at the clock.

"I'm heading for the office for a few minutes and then to bed," he announced. "It's darn late and it's been a hard day and night."

"I'll walk with you," Slade offered. "I'll be back shortly, Marie."

"Please do," she replied. "I'm through for the night," she added, casting him a glance through her lashes.

"I doubt it," chuckled the sheriff. Marie blushed and made a face at him.

Still chuckling, Medford stood up, plucked Slade's well worn "J.B." from the peg on which it hung and donned it. The broad-brimmed rainshed dropped down to rest on his rather prominent ears. Going along with the joke, Slade gravely perched the sheriff's old brown derby on the top of his head. Marie trilled musical laughter.

"You both look so silly," she said. There was a turning of heads and chuckles from the bar and the tables.

"We're making a hit," said Medford. "We should do this more often."

He soberly led the way to the swinging doors, Slade striding a little behind him.

They passed through the doors with the sheriff still a bit in front.

Hardly had the doors swung shut when Slade flung out a long arm and slammed the sheriff against the building wall as a gun blazed, and another, from the dark mouth of a narrow alley almost directly across the street, going sideways in the same ripple of movement. Medford gave a grunt, reeled and fell.

Both Slade's Colts let go with a rattling crash. A cry echoed the reports and the body of a man plunged out of the alley onto the sidewalk. There sounded a patter of footsteps.

Slade leaped forward, but past him rushed half a dozen young Mexicans from the cantina. They tore into the alley, going like the wind. There was the sound of a shot, blending with a horrible gurgling shriek, then silence.

Slade turned to the sheriff, who was scrambling to his feet, hatless, rubbing his head and swearing profusely.

"Where'd it get you?" *El Halcón* asked anxiously.

"Head," sputtered the sheriff. "Darn near knocked me silly, but I don't feel any blood."

A swift examination showed no wound

other than a swelling lump. Slade picked up his fallen hat, glanced at it and passed it to the sheriff without speaking.

The heavy metal buckle that held the band in place was bent and twisted.

"Slug hit the buckle, which deflected it, but slammed the buckle against your head, giving you quite a whack," Slade explained. "Guess you're sort of in debt to that old buckle.

"And if we hadn't changed hats like we did, for a joke, I might well have gotten my comeuppance," he added. "This old derby is in the way of being your trade mark — you always wear it — and they aimed at the one of us wearing the rainshed, which happened to be you."

"And if you didn't think and act like a lightning flash, I'd have gotten it, all right," declared the sheriff. "Here come the boys back," he added as the young Mexicans filed from the alley without so much as a glance at the body sprawled on the sidewalks. "And look, Pancho's wiping his knife. Did you find out who it was, Pancho?"

Pancho shrugged with Latin eloquence. "*Los muertos no hablan* — the dead do not talk —" he replied. "My blade is swift, and my cast does not miss. It sped home before the *ladrone* pulled trigger; his shot went wild."

The patrons of the cantina were boiling into the street volleying questions and curses in two languages. Marie was beside Slade, clinging to his arm with her little hands.

"If I let you out of my sight for an instant you get into trouble!" she stormed. "Heavenly days! What next?"

"Everything under control," Slade replied, patting her shoulder. "Go back in. I'll be with you in a minute. Tell somebody to fetch a light."

She did as he said and a bracket lamp was quickly forthcoming. Slade took it and led the way across the street. "Let's see what we bagged," he said to the sheriff.

The dead man on the sidewalk was blocky in build with a leathery face and muddy-looking brown eyes. He was garbed in rangeland clothes.

"Never saw him before," said Medford. "Maybe better luck with the one Pancho got."

But after glancing at the face of the second drygulcher, who was tall and scrawny and nondescript of countenance, he again shook his head.

"Border scum, gun-for-hire," was Slade's

verdict. Pancho plucked at his sleeve.

"*Capitan,* I have seen both before," he muttered softly. "In Nuevo Laredo, across the river. The chief of police ordered both out of town a while back. They were trying to rob a drunken man. Had they not been *Americanos,* he would have locked them in the calaboose."

"And they got hired to do a little chore over here," Slade said thoughtfully. "Well, I'm afraid they won't collect their pay."

The pockets of the drygulchers discovered nothing of significance save a good deal of money. Medford glanced inquiringly at Slade, who grinned and slipped it into Pancho's hand. The Mexican chuckled, winked at his companions, and headed for the cantina.

The crowd was thinning out. Miguel paused beside the sheriff.

"I'll have some of my *muchachos* carry the carcasses to your office," he ordered.

"That'll be fine, and much obliged, Mig," the sheriff accepted.

"Oh, my gosh!" he suddenly wailed as Miguel hurried away on his errand.

"Now what?" Slade asked.

"I just remembered what I'm packin' in my pocket," Medford moaned. "If the slug had hit *that!* Gentlemen, hush!"

"Lucky you didn't fall on the dynamite side," Slade smiled.

"If I had!" gulped the sheriff. "If I had! I'm headin' for the office and lock the blasted stuff up before something does happen. Here come Miguel's boys with a couple shutters to pack the carcasses on. Give me my derby. I'll buy a new buckle for your rainshed. Would sorta like to keep the old one for a souvenir."

"Okay," Slade said and passed him the derby and donned his own broad-brim. "We'll talk over this business later; I want to think on it a bit."

"Right," said Medford. "Now you better hustle inside before Marie has a conniption duck fit, and who could blame her! Be seeing you."

When Slade entered the cantina, Marie had changed her dancing costume for a street dress and was awaiting him. Old Miguel beamed happily as they left together.

5

The Montezuma was similar to the Crosby House in Beaumont in that everybody who was anybody in the Laredo section, and quite a few that weren't, sooner or later showed up in the Montezuma. When Slade dropped in, shortly after noon, he found Sheriff Medford surrounding a hefty helping of chuck.

"Still get the shakes every time I think about that blasted bundle of dynamite," announced the sheriff, waving his fork. "Sit down and have a snort or something."

"Think I'll settle for coffee," Slade replied, occupying a chair. Medford jerked a thumb as if physically propelling a nearby waiter to the table.

"Well, what do you think about things, especially what happened last night?" he asked.

"For one thing," Slade answered, "that there is a ruthless, able and well organized bunch working to delay or nullify the irrigation project, and unless they're stopped they may do just that. Eastern capital is becoming a mite jittery."

"And from what happened down on Grant Street last night, I've a prime notion that somebody else is becoming a mite jittery," said the sheriff. "Reckon they don't take kind to *El Halcón* all of a sudden showing up in the section. Do you figure it's the cattlemen responsible for what's going on?"

"It is not beyond the realm of possibility that the cattlemen favor it," Slade replied slowly. "However, the things that happened last night were not the work of range riders, but of somebody who knows his business. Quite a few somebodies, I'd say. The chore done on the Albemarle safe was the work of an expert. And the try at burning the material steamer comes into the same category. Both chores were smoothly handled, and were it not for the lucky chance that the fire department was right there on the job, the steamer would have burned."

"And if it weren't for you and your seeing things other folks would overlook, the other chore would have been a plumb success, with somebody blown to Hades," the sheriff commented. "To say nothing of that nice little try at drygulching from the alley. How

52

in blazes did you catch on to that so fast."

"Saw a shadow move in the alley mouth and didn't like the looks of it," Slade explained. "I have a habit of keeping an eye on alley mouths. Drygulchers usually run to a pattern and they seem to consider alley mouths excellent set-ups for a sneak killing. However, they almost always forget one small detail that may well be their undoing. Even when the lighting is poor, they are shadows against a bank of deeper shadows which to an extent throws back what light there is and renders them visible."

"Uh-huh, for eyes like yours," grunted the sheriff. "I didn't see anything."

"I've a notion you were not looking for anything," Slade said. "I was. I studied that alley when I was here before and concluded it was set at a nice angle to cover the cantina door. So I never step completely out onto the street without glancing toward it, as last night."

Medford shook his head. "I don't know how the devil you do it," he sighed wearily. "You seem to think of everything before it has time to happen."

"In Ranger work you learn to think of everything and to endeavor to anticipate it, if you wish to stay alive," Slade replied.

"Guess that's so," Medford agreed. "Anyhow, you sure don't miss much.

"Hello!" he exclaimed. "Here comes somebody who is a sorta big jigger with the project."

Slade who, as usual, was continually studying the occupants of the room and at the same time watching the door, had already noted the newcomer's entrance.

"That's Amos Rolf," the sheriff elaborated. "He's purchasing agent for the outfit and seems to have something to say about most everything. He's tough and smart and knows his business. Personally inspects every shipment that comes in and if it don't 'pear just right to him, back it goes pronto. He looked over that steamer's cargo this morning. Said there was very little damage 'cept by water and that that didn't 'mount to much, seeing as it is mostly heavy equipment and steel beams. Said if she'd gone to the bottom, though, it would have seriously delayed the project."

Amos Rolf had a rugged, composed face and an authoritative manner. He was a big man, slightly under six feet, Slade estimated, but powerfully, almost massively built, with huge hands. His hair was dark, lightly sprinkled with gray, a premature gray, Slade felt, judging his age to be not much more than thirty. His eyes were also dark, and very bright. They swept the room in an all-embracing glance before he made his way to the bar.

"Looks competent, and there's sure plenty of him," the Ranger commented.

"Yep, he's all of that," Medford nodded. "Not a bad sort. Don't talk much but is pleasant. Doesn't seem to take much interest in anything except his work."

"I imagine he has plenty to keep him occupied," Slade said. "Even without the continual threat of trouble of some sort or another."

"So I gather," the sheriff agreed. "Nigh as bad as being a peace officer and packin' dynamite in a pocket. I still ain't got over that."

"You will," Slade assured him smilingly. "Be all set for the next time."

"There ain't going to be any next time," Medford declared emphatically. "Next time *you'll* pack it. Then if it goes off . . ."

"The results will be the same, if you happen to be in my company," Slade interrupted, his smile broadening.

The sheriff snorted, sampled his drink and refrained from further comment.

"By the way, did anybody recognize those two bodies?" Slade asked.

Medford shook his head. "If they did they

wouldn't admit it," he replied. "I've a notion, from what Pancho said last night, the hellions mostly hung out in Nuevo Laredo, across the river, before they got chased outa there."

"Quite likely," Slade conceded. "You might check the various racks and stables for a couple of unclaimed horses. They might possibly tell us something, although it is doubtful.

"I wonder if they could have belonged to the bunch I met on the trail," he added thoughtfully. "*They* could have circled around and returned to town after dividing their loot and deciding that they had nothing to fear here."

"And figured, after hearing about what didn't happen at the Albemarle office, that you had something to do with preventing that," Medford surmised shrewdly.

"I would say somebody figured that, after what happened on Grant Street last night," Slade replied.

"And if so, you're on a real nice spot," the sheriff commented. Slade shrugged.

"Been on spots before," he replied cheerfully. "The important thing is not to be on the spot at the wrong time."

"I don't believe you've got a nerve in your body, as I've said before," Medford growled.

"Sometimes I figure you really enjoy dodging lead."

"There's considerable satisfaction in *dodging* it," Slade countered. "It's not dodging it that's unpleasant."

The sheriff grunted disgustedly and called for another snort. Slade ordered more coffee.

"Doc Beard going to hold an inquest on those bodies?" Slade asked. "Guess he's still coroner, eh?"

"Yep, he's still coroner and figures on an inquest tomorrow afternoon," the sheriff answered. "Guess he calc'lates he has to do something to earn his pay. You can admit downing one of the horned toads, of course, but I've a notion it would be a good notion to keep Pancho out of it."

"Yes, no sense in advertising the part he played," Slade agreed. "No reason why he should get mixed up in the feud just because he did me a good turn."

"Guess there's something to being *El Halcón,* after all," said Medford. "Besides having plenty of enemies, you've got plenty of good friends in all sorts of places."

"Yes, and that's important," Slade said soberly.

The sheriff chuckled. "The boys sure got on the job fast last night," he observed.

"Reckon soon as they heard the shooting they figured *El Halcón* was mixed up in it somehow and might need a hand."

"They were grouped close to the door — they always are, six or seven of them, and it didn't take them long to figure things correctly," Slade replied. "Yes, they moved fast. That bunch, or most of them, were reared by the mountain Yaquis and running is an exercise much practiced by the Yaquis. That hellion hadn't a chance to outrun them to the other end of the alley, even though he had a start. And Pancho can split the mark on an ace-card at twenty paces with his sticker. He's quite an artist with a blade."

"Evidently, as I've a notion that sidewinder is telling the devil about now," Medford agreed dryly.

Glancing toward the bar, Slade noted that Amos Rolf, the purchasing agent for the irrigation project, was holding converse with John Gorty, the owner. Rolf did not turn, but Gorty twice glanced toward the table occupied by the sheriff and himself. Slade shrewdly surmised that he was the topic of conversation, which doubtless dealt with the happenings of the night before. Which wasn't strange; only natural that Rolf would be interested.

That his guess was right was proven a few

minutes later when the pair approached the table. Gorty performed the introductions. Rolf shook hands with a good grip and smiled quite pleasantly.

"Been hearing quite a bit about you, Mr. Slade," he said. "Hope you'll see fit to be with us for quite a while. Ride down to the project when you find the time and look things over. Imagine you'll find it interesting, even though a bit confusing for a cattleman."

"I'll do that, Mr. Rolf," Slade promised. "Yes, I imagine it is interesting even to one ignorant of the details." Sheriff Medford bit back a grin with difficulty.

After a few more words, Rolf took his leave. "Got to get back on the job," he said. "Come to town to look over that steamer damaged by fire. Not too much damage, I'm glad to say." With a wave of his hand, he left the saloon.

After Gorty had ambled back to the bar, Medford let the grin spread.

"Ignorant of the details!" he scoffed. "And you one of the best engineers in Texas."

"I fear you overestimate my ability," Slade smiled.

"And I suppose old Jim Dunn, who runs the C. & P. Railroad System right up to the hilt, underestimates you, too, eh?" the sheriff retorted dryly. "Saw him over at Sanderson a little while back; you know I've known him for years. He gave me to understand that you did him a mighty big favor not long ago; he can't talk enough about you. He swears there's not a better engineer in Texas, and Jim Dunn always knows what he's talking about."

C. & P. General Manager James G. "Jaggers" Dunn was right. Shortly before the death of his father, which followed financial reverses that cost the elder Slade his ranch, young Walt had graduated from a noted college of engineering. He had planned to take a post graduate course in special subjects to round out his education and better fit him for the profession he had determined to make his life's work.

This becoming impossible for the time being, he lent an attentive ear when Captain Jim McNelty, with whom he had worked some during summer vacations, suggested that he sign up with the Rangers for a while and pursue his studies in spare time.

Long since, he had gotten more from private study than he could have hoped for from the postgrad. But meanwhile Ranger work had gotten a strong hold on him, providing as it did so many opportunities to do good, to help deserving people and to make the land he loved a better place to live.

So he hesitated to sever connections with the illustrious body of law enforcement officers. He was young, plenty of time to be an engineer. He'd stick with the Rangers for a while. He had received more than one offer of lucrative employment from influential persons he had contacted in the course of his Ranger activities, including one from General Manager Dunn. And he had found his knowledge of engineering valuable on certain occasions. Somehow, he had a feeling that the present might be an example.

"Yep, Dunn is right," the sheriff repeated. He chuckled. "Reckon Rolf would be a mite surprised did he know the truth about you."

"He doesn't need to know, or anybody else hereabouts, so far as I can see," Slade replied. "Sometimes the less folks know about one the better."

"Guess that's so," Medford conceded. "Now what?"

Slade glanced at the clock. "Still quite a few hours till sundown," he remarked. "Believe I'll accept Rolf's invitation and ride down to the project and look things over. As he said, it should be interesting. It's a big chore, with plenty of difficulties attendant. According to the plans, it will run for miles both above and below here and they'll have problems to solve.

"The Rio Grande's flow is very erratic, varying from slight flow to six hundred thousand cubic feet a second. It may be but a trickle around El Paso and a roaring flood here. It is essentially a storm water stream subject to great and sudden floods and to extreme fluctuations in its volume. This must be taken into consideration and provision against it be made.

"The flood season is usually August and September for this section and then water must be stored for irrigation. Otherwise, during the dry season, the crops will burn up. Water must be impounded against the period of drought when the river is too low to adequately supply the lead channels. And there must be proper drainage facilities to take care of the flood season or the crops will be drowned out. It's not just a matter of digging ditches and letting the water run out of the river onto the lands to be irrigated."

"Sounds too complicated for me," grunted the sheriff. "Reckon it's all plumb clear to you, though."

Slade laughed. "Oh, it's not so bad as it sounds," he said. "But it's not exactly simple." His eyes grew thoughtful.

"I've a notion about something I don't believe anybody else has thought of," he added. "I may get a chance to put it into effect. Never can tell. I'm here as a Ranger, but before now I've gotten mixed up in something that appeared extraneous to the chore I had to do, but sooner or later tied in nicely and simplified the chore."

"Oh, you'll figure something to give folks the creeps and send some hellions skalley-hootin'," the sheriff predicted. "Never knew you to fail."

Slade laughed again and headed for the stable where Shadow had his abode for the time being.

"Nope, horse, you never can tell," he told the big black as he cinched the hull into place. Anyhow, we'll go have us a little look-see. Give you a chance to stretch your legs a mite, at least, and that won't make you paw sod."

Shadow rolled his eyes and did not deign even a snort in reply. His whole attitude seemed to say:

"Here we go again!"

6

Slade chuckled and rode east on Matamoros Street. He sloshed through the shallow trickle of Zacate Creek and continued on his way toward where the start of the irrigation project was gaining impetus.

Yes, it was a giant undertaking end when completed would change a great many square miles of semi-arid terrain into fertile farming land. Slade could envision the springing crops, the homes, the prosperous little settlements where now was little more than a wilderness.

And it would be worth while, bringing happiness and content to many. He was glad that he might possibly play a part in its consummation. Greed and corruption might well exist for a while. In fact, recent events pointed to the presence of those vices. But he was confident that in the end right would prevail. He rode on, humming gaily in his deep, rich voice, to where was a scene of ant-like activity.

Down around Brownsville, near the mouth of the river, the Rio Grande, winding between muddy banks at the city's southern boundary, had through centuries deposited the silt that made the town the center of a rich delta of citrus orchards, vegetable farms and cotton fields. What irrigation was needed was simple, for there the great river was dependable.

Here it was different; there was no deposit of silt to speak of. The river rushed between high end steep banks, at times but a shallow stream, at others a roaring flood. Which made irrigation a decidedly complicated affair.

As he neared the scene of operations, Slade was impressed by the efficiency displayed and the fact that most modern methods were being employed.

Everywhere was bustling activity and orderly confusion. The air quivered to the thudding of pile drivers, the gouging of steam shovels and the chatter of air compressors. The work was going ahead apace and, barring the unforeseen, the project should progress per schedule. But Slade had an uneasy premonition that the "unforeseen" might well play havoc with well laid plans. The undertaking was vulnerable in many instances, did someone with knowledge and efficiency take advantage of conditions that were bound to develop. Well, he was here for the purpose of frustrating such attempts. He shrugged his broad shoulders and rode on.

In the shade of a convenient tree, where grass grew, he drew rein and dismounted. Flipping out the bit and loosening the cinches, he left Shadow to his own devices. Strolling forward on foot, he approached the scene of operations.

Nearby, a ponderous "hydraulic giant" was battering down banks of gravel preparatory to the construction of an impounding basin. The giant had a nozzle with a double joint that could be turned in a horizontal and in a vertical plane. A stream of water under high pressure provided by a big air compressor was directed against the banks. Such a giant spouted fifty cubic feet per second. Under the terrific beat of the jet, the hard-packed gravel dissolved like sugar. Efficient and fast.

Slade moved a little closer, almost to where the thick stream hissed through the air, for the operation interested him. He glanced toward the gravel bank, flickered a glance back toward the nozzle-man — and went sideways in a cat-like leap. The whistling steel-hard jet barely brushed his side. Had it struck him squarely it would have killed him.

"Look out!" the nozzle-man yelled belatedly.

Slade turned to face him, took a long stride forward.

"The — the nozzle slipped," the man stuttered. Slade let the full force of his cold eyes rest on the fellow's face. And they were the terrible eyes of *El Halcón.* Under the menace in those icy eyes, the nozzle-man whitened visibly. Slade spoke five evenly spaced words:

"Don't — let — it — slip — again!"

"I — I won't," the man mumbled.

From nearby sounded a stentorian roar. Amos Rolf, the purchasing agent, came plowing toward the nozzle-man, his face convulsed with anger.

"You clumsy idiot!" he stormed at the nozzle-man. "What are you trying to do, kill somebody?"

"I — I slipped, Mr. Rolf," the fellow mouthed.

"Yes, I guess you did!" Rolf retorted sarcastically. "Handle that thing properly, before somebody gets hurt."

"I will, Mr. Rolf," the man replied, looking frightened. Rolf turned to the Ranger.

"I'm sorry this had to happen, Mr. Slade," he said. "An example of why there are so many industrial accidents. Plain awkward carelessness."

"No harm done, and accidents will happen," Slade returned lightly.

But *El Halcón* knew well it had been no *accident.* The man had deliberately shifted the jointed nozzle the merest trifle, in the horizontal plane. *No accident, just an attempt at snake-blooded murder!*

"Come along, Mr. Slade, and I'll show you around," Rolf invited, with a final glare at the nozzle-man. "Maybe together we can stay in one piece, although I won't promise for sure, the things we have to put up with from incompetents."

They set out together, and very quickly, Slade became convinced that Rolf was thoroughly grounded in all the principles of irrigation. He pointed out interesting angles and discussed them with familiarity and in a manner not difficult for a layman to follow. However, now and then becoming somewhat technical in his explanation —

"Drainage is one of the problems we'll have to cope with here, because of the fluctuations of the river providing the water supply. What will be necessary in the dry season would drown out the crops in time of flood. Drains must be deep enough that capillary action will not bring water to the surface to evaporate and deposit alkalies injurious to plant life.

"I fear this sounds like jargon to you," he added apologetically.

"I find it interesting and portrayed very clearly," Slade replied. "Even one ignorant of such matters can fairly well follow you."

Rolf smiled and nodded and went on with his explanations. But as he talked, and indicated certain salient features, Slade's black brows drew together slightly, the concentration furrow between them deepening. A sign that *El Halcón* was doing some thinking.

"Here comes somebody I want you to meet," Rolf said suddenly. "Mr. Ernest Clark, the construction engineer in charge. A nice person."

As the engineer drew near, Slade was inclined to agree with Rolf's estimate. Ernest Clark was a pleasant-faced man of somewhat under middle age. He had clear eyes that Slade thought were a trifle dreamy, but his movements were alert and vigorous. He was close to six feet tall, lean and well set up. He shook hands with a grip that was firm but not too firm when Rolf performed the introductions.

"Mr. Slade is one of Sheriff Medford's friends and rode down to look things over," Rolf explained.

"I hope you found your visit interesting, Mr. Slade," Clark smiled.

"I have, very," Slade said, and meant it.

"Those I-beams I had sent you, Clark, were satisfactory," Rolf stated rather than asked.

"Perfectly," Clark replied.

"And the new compressor. I had some changes made that I think will better its performance."

"Undoubtedly," Clark instantly agreed.

As they talked, Slade quickly got the impression that Clark deferred to the purchasing agent, despite the importance of his own position. Well, it wasn't too strange. Amos Rolf was without doubt a dominant personality.

A little later, Slade glanced at the westering sun. "Guess I'd better be getting back to town," he announced. "Thank you for everything, Mr. Rolf. And you, Mr. Clark. Hope to see you both again soon."

"We'll see you in town, perhaps tonight," Rolf replied. "I sorta like the bright lights. Ernest here is a good deal of a hermit. Shuts himself up with his books when it gets dark."

"I fear I'm the retiring sort, Mr. Slade,"

Clark said with a smile.

Walt Slade was very thoughtful as he rode to town through the blue and gold beauty of the dusk. So whoever was kicking up the rukus in the section had key men mixed in with the project workers. The nozzle-man was an example. He could do plenty of damage with his powerful machine did he handle it ineptly.

"He's an expert, all right, and would quite probably make it appear an accident or a mechanical defect, that most likely," Slade told his horse. "Evidently the hellion recognized me as *El Halcón* and figured it was a good chance to get rid of me. Came close to putting it over, too. If I hadn't seen the glint of light as he turned that nozzle the merest fraction, I'd have gotten that stream amidships. Would have been like being hit by a battering ram. Well, it didn't quite work, and that's all that counts."

Shadow appeared to nod sober agreement. His expression seemed to say:

"Uh-huh, and anybody with just average good eyesight would never have caught on. Certainly wouldn't have reacted properly in time. Oh, you're part cat, all right, and almost as good at thinking and acting fast as a horse."

At which last, *El Halcón* chuckled. Immediately, however, his eyes grew thoughtful.

"Horse," he said, "I'm very much of the opinion that Mr. Clark, the construction engineer in charge of the project, slipped a mite. Perhaps due to lack of knowledge of the vagaries of this confounded river. His lead channels are not deep enough and not properly gradiated. He'll never get the needed head of water during a real dry spell. And I'm also suspicious of his laterals; they don't look just right to me.

"What to do about it? I'm hanged if I know, at the moment. I can hardly approach him and correct him without revealing a lot more about myself than I care to do right now. This will require quite a bit of thinking out. Anyhow, we are here not to regulate irrigation projects but to bring certain law breakers to justice. So june along and don't paw sod."

Slade's habit of relegating expression-speech to his horse was not mere idle past-time. Instead, it was in the nature of an analyzing and clarifying of his own thought processes, employing the medium of imaginary equine understanding and response. And really, taking Shadow's undoubted intelligence into consideration, he was never quite sure but that the horse did understand

72

and was able, to an extent at least, to equate his own mental reactions so that his master's brain cells would, subconsciously, perhaps, be receptive.

Be that as it may, it was good to talk to his horse at times, especially when pondering a knotty problem. Something frequently indulged in by men who ride alone.

7

Arriving in Laredo, he cared for Shadow and then repaired to the Montezuma, where he hoped to find Sheriff Medford, with whom he wished to discuss the recent happenings.

It was the sheriff's regular eating time and as he expected, Slade found him ensconced behind a hefty surrounding. After giving his own order, he regaled the peace officer with an account of the day's misadventures.

"After you hot and heavy, eh?" Medford growled, biting savagely into a hunk of steak. After swallowing which, he said several things best not repeated. "Yes, after you hot and heavy, the blankety-blanks."

"Looks sort of that way," Slade replied lightly. "Anyhow, I've a gent to keep an eye out for, that nozzle-man; he might just possibly lead me to somebody more important."

"You should have plugged the sidewinder," said Medford.

"I think I at least gave him something of a scare," Slade said. "He looked it. And I'm sure Rolf did. I thought for a minute Rolf was going to take him apart. I guess he thought so, too, from his expression. I've a notion Rolf is a bad man to go up against."

"Looks it, all right," the sheriff agreed.

"He sure was in a temper with that fellow," Slade added. "His eyes were like a mad cat's."

"Couldn't blame him," grunted Medford. "He knows what one of those jets would do to a man if it hit him square; would have knocked you right into the Judgment Day."

"He seems to know more than a little about the irrigation business," Slade said thoughtfully. "Sort of forgot himself, I'd say, and went into technical language which would be so much gibberish to a layman. Apologized for it immediately afterward."

"Well, I reckon he has to know a good deal about it to hold the job he has," the sheriff commented.

"He knows a lot more than one would expect from a purchasing agent, whose concern is the condition of the goods he buys. And somehow, I felt that Clark, the engineer, was ready and willing to accept his opinion on anything. He might own a large block of stock in the project, of course, and have considerable say as to what is and isn't done."

"Could be," agreed the sheriff.

"Well, he's not our problem, so let him and Clark settle it between themselves," Slade concluded. "Our chore is to put a stop to the heck raising hereabouts, find out who's responsible and bring him, or several hims, which is more likely, to justice. Our big concern is who the devil it can be."

"And speaking of the devil!" exclaimed Medford. "There's a feller just come in I've been keeping an eye on and wondering about a mite."

"Yes?" Slade prompted. "Who is he?"

"Name's Beckley, Dick Beckley," the sheriff replied. "Bought the Triangle spread, a good holding, from old Winfield Cunningham, who moved east, not long after you were here last. Been sort of a burr under the bull's tail ever since. First off he fenced some of his holding with barbed wire, which didn't set well with the oldtimers, and ran sheep onto his hill pastures, which didn't set well, either."

"Barbed wire is coming to this section, just as it has in other parts of Texas and the oldtimers might as well get used to it, and sheep are all right if they are handled as they should be and not allowed to destroy range," Slade interpolated.

The sheriff, himself an oldtime cattleman, did not appear overly impressed. However, he merely grunted and resumed his dissertation on Richard Beckley:

"Next the young hellion got to rummaging about in a bunch of papers Cunningham left in the ranchhouse, some of which belonged to Cunningham's grandfather. He hit on an old Spanish grant that sorta 'peared to give him title to a stretch of land the irrigation people had bought. He brought suit. The irrigation folks fought back and the thing is still hanging fire in the courts. Beckley has kinda hinted at bribery and collusion, though I guess he's never come right out and said so. But he's sure got no use for the irrigation bunch and makes no bones of saying so. Overbearing sort of coot and seems to rub most everybody the wrong way. I know Amos Rolf don't cotton to him. They had words in here one night, but Gorty and his floor men busted it up before they could start real trouble. Rolf left and Beckley promised to behave himself and did."

Slade nodded thoughtfully and gave attention to the young rancher.

Beckley had a hard-lined face, a well formed but tight mouth and flashing black eyes. His hair was tawny, worn rather long, and inclined to curl. His bearing was aggressive to the verge of swagger and he swung his big shoulders as he walked. He gave the appearance, Slade thought, of intelligence above the average. Looked to be a hard man and probably was.

"Would have been quite a set-to if him and Rolf had really got together," the sheriff remarked. "He's a bit taller than Rolf but I don't think he's as heavy."

"Know where he came from and what he did before he landed here?" Slade asked.

"Understand he's from the Sabine River country," Medford replied, adding with apparent irrelevance, "lots of tough hellions come from over there. Gather he worked on a spread there and saved some money, or had some, and decided to settle here. Don't talk much about himself. He brought a bunch of hands with him — hard lookin' characters who don't talk much either and mostly stick together. Seem to behave themselves, though. Always 'pear to have plenty of money, and they spend it."

Which last remark caused Slade to smile slightly, intimating as it did that the Triangle C bunch had more spending money than could be expected from cowhand wages.

Medford apparently read what was passing through the Ranger's mind, for he grinned a trifle sheepishly.

"All that, of course, don't mean there's anything wrong with Beckley and his hellions," he hastened to admit. "Just the same, though, I can't help doing a mite of thinking. Beckley don't wish the irrigation project well, that's plumb sure for certain."

"But doesn't necessarily mean that he would go to such lengths as felonious sabotage and attempted murder to slow up the project or express his resentment," Slade pointed out. "As to his alleged hints of bribery or collusion, he might have been misunderstood or was just making big medicine. And as you said, the matter of controversy between him and the irrigation people is pending in the courts and he has no way of knowing which way the cat will jump. The decision might well be in his favor. I gather the irrigation people challenged the authenticity of the grant, but that does not mean they will come out on top. As you well know, many such grants have been upheld by Texas courts."

"So you figure Beckley out of it?"

"I didn't say that," Slade denied. "I merely outlined the case as it stands relative to Beckley. I don't know who is responsible for what has happened, and until I do know, anybody with any interest in the business is suspect. That is my attitude as a Ranger. My big problem at the moment is to ascertain the motive. Find the motive and you are well on the way to corraling your man. One might say that Beckley is motivated by animosity toward the irrigation people, but it is not necessarily so."

"I reckon you're right," sighed the sheriff. "Trying to keep up with you is like trying to run down a scared coyote with a wooden leg."

Slade chuckled and ordered coffee, meanwhile studying Richard Beckley, who was toying with a glass and staring moodily into the back bar mirror.

"Look where the young hellion got to," Medford suddenly snorted. "All those jiggers at the far end of the bar are irrigation workers, so he had to shoulder right in alongside of them, with plenty of other room at the bar right now. Blazes! here come half a dozen of his bunch!"

Slade had already noted the group of cowhands pushing through the swinging doors. They were hard looking rannies, all right, lean alert men of confident bearing. Their garb was conventional rangeland wear and they all packed guns. They streamed down the bar and gathered alongside and behind their boss, who turned and engaged them in conversation. One, Slade noticed, carried his left arm in a sling. Abruptly he asked a question,

"Where is Beckley's holding located?"

"About six miles to the east of here," Medford replied. Slade nodded, and although the sheriff glanced at him interrogatively, did not follow up the question with explanatory comment.

"There's going to be trouble," the sheriff muttered. "Betcha there's going to be trouble; those hellions are looking at each other."

"Quite likely," Slade conceded and moved his chair back from the table, meanwhile watching the two groups closely.

The irrigation bunch, brawny, rugged men, had drawn together in a close knot; they did not seem to be looking for trouble, although they would doubtless not pull away from it did it come their way. They sipped their glasses and evidently tried to ignore the cowhands.

But Beckley, inflamed by his drinks, appeared goaded by a demon of perversity. He kept casting sneering glances toward the project men, and making remarks to his companions.

It was hard to tell who started it. The irrigation men blamed the cowhands. The cowhands blamed the irrigation men. John Gorty blamed both, and the sheriff agreed with him.

Anyhow, it erupted with the explosive suddenness of an overpowered geyser.

Gorty and his floor men bellowed forward, and were engulfed in the wild tangle of fists and feet. Chairs went to matchwood. Tables were overturned, bottles knocked from the bar. The hanging lamps jumped and quivered to the uproar.

The cowhand whose arm was in a sling hurled himself into the fray, striking with his right, and suddenly got one on his injured member. He gave a howl of pain and reeled back and back until he was clear of the whirling melee. His face convulsed, he jerked his gun and swung it toward the man who struck him.

The lamps jumped to the crash of a shot. The injured man howled again, wringing his blood streaming fingers. His gun, the lock smashed, lay on the floor a dozen feet distant.

Slade's voice rolled in thunder through the room.

"Hold it! That will be all!"

The fighting ceased. Both groups swung around to stare askance at the grim figure facing them. Slade had a gun in each hand, one wisping smoke. His icy eyes dominated both groups. The wounded man moaned and gagged.

Sheriff Medford was also on his feet, gun out.

"It had better be all!" he bawled. "I'll fill the calaboose with the crowd of you terrapin-brained blankety-blanks!"

Confident that hostilities were at an end, for the time being at least, Slade holstered his Colts and sauntered forward.

"Let me see your hand," he told the wounded man, who, looking a bit white and sick, extended it.

"Nothing to it," Slade said, after a brief examination. "Bit of meat knocked off is all." He turned to the swearing owner, who was nursing a blackening eye.

"Gorty," he said, "I suppose you have bandage and some salve in the back room, right? Okay, get them and I'll tie up this jigger."

"A double dose of arsenic would be better," growled Gorty. "But okay if you say so, Mr. Slade." With a glare at the wounded puncher, he headed for the back room.

Very quickly, Slade had the slight wound treated and bandaged. He noted there was a stain on the puncher's upper shirt sleeve of his left arm but did not comment.

"Now see if you can behave yourself before you really get hurt," he told the cowboy, giving the bandage a final pat. "You ought to be ashamed of yourself."

"Sorry, feller," said the puncher. "When that hellion whacked my arm it hurt like the devil and I reckon I sorta lost my head. Cow stuck a horn through it yesterday."

Slade gathered that he meant through the arm, not his head. He nodded and accepted the explanation for what it was worth, which was probably not much.

"It's all right, don't bother about it," the puncher vouchsafed in addition. Slade nodded again and refrained from examining the limb.

Dick Beckley, who had been staring at Slade in silence, suddenly spoke.

"Feller, do you always hit things that way?" he asked.

"Sometimes I miss — *inside* the gun-hand," Slade replied. Beckley blinked. The wounded man winced.

As he turned away, Slade's keen ears caught the murmur of one of the cowboys.

" 'The fastest gun in the whole Southwest!' Guess it's so."

The two groups sullenly drew apart, nursing their wounds, which were not serious.

Gorty, the owner, gave them a sound tongue lashing, ably abetted by the sheriff, leaving the erstwhile battlers decidedly subdued. Slade returned to his table, where Medford shortly joined him.

"Well, looks like you prevented a killing," he remarked to the Ranger.

"Possibly," Slade conceded.

"Seems to me I recall you shooting a gun out of a horned toad's hand like that once before," the sheriff commented.

"Yes, I did," Slade admitted. "It was a more difficult shot, for I had to take the chance of missing and plugging somebody. This time it was easy. The fellow reeled back after he was hit until only the bar was behind him, and the bartenders were out of the way. Quite simple with a good light and at that distance."

"Uh-huh, quite simple, for *El Halcón,*" the sheriff said dryly. "I wouldn't have wanted to take that chance, and I'm considered purty good with an iron. Say, come to think of it, why'd you want to know where Beckley's holding is located?"

"When I had the brush with that bunch on the trail last night, I'm pretty sure I got one of them in the arm," Slade replied. "That fellow over there said a cow stuck its horn through it, but he didn't seem to want

85

me to examine it, although the bleeding had started afresh. Just set me to wondering a mite."

"And you figure —" the sheriff began.

"I figure nothing," Slade interrupted. "Perhaps the fellow was telling the truth, and anyhow there's nothing to definitely tie him up with that bunch the other night. Just something in the nature of a coincidence, and interesting."

"Yes, darned interesting," Medford growled, casting a glowering glance toward the far end of the bar, where cowhands and irrigation workers were devoting their attention to their drinks and, to all appearances, paying one another no mind.

"But don't go jumping at conclusions," Slade cautioned. "All this approaches too close to the obvious, and I've learned to distrust the obvious."

8

Shortly afterward, the irrigation workers departed, filing past the cowhands with compressed lips and menacing eyes, but offering no violence.

"Guess that's all for tonight," observed the sheriff. "Beckley and his bunch 'pear considerable cooled down. Just the same, though, I'm ambling out to keep an eye on those other hellions. They might take a notion to round up reinforcements and come back."

"I doubt it, but go ahead if it'll make you feel better."

"What you aim to do?" Medford asked as he stood up.

"I'm going down to Miguel's cantina shortly," Slade replied.

"Okay," said the sheriff, "but watch your step."

After the sheriff passed through the swinging doors, Slade ordered more coffee, rolled a cigarette and relaxed comfortably, now and then regarding Beckley and his hands.

No doubt but they knew him for *El Halcón.* But just what effect it would have on them he couldn't say. Anyhow, he now had somebody to keep an eye on for a while other than the nozzle-man. Business was picking up a mite.

He studied the faces of the bunch, listened to snatches of conversation his keen ears could catch during lulls of the general uproar, and arrived at no definite conclusion.

Beckley's riders gave the appearance of being regulation cowhands, and as such would be unlikely to possess the technical knowledge that marked the perpetration of the atrocities committed. But you never could tell for sure. Men are not always what they look and act to be, and cowhands sometimes turned to other pursuits. And he couldn't afford to overlook any leads, no matter how slender. His judgment must be held in abeyance until something happened or he learned something that would tend to crystallize it.

Slade had noted Beckley glancing in his direction from time to time and he was not particularly surprised when the Triangle C owner disengaged himself from the group and approached his table.

"Mind if I join you for a few minutes, Mr. Slade?" he asked.

"Not at all," the Ranger replied. "Have a chair." He beckoned a waiter. Beckley, who appeared decidedly sobered, shook his head to decline the proffered drink.

"I wish to thank you, Mr. Slade, for what you did," he said. "Chuck Perkins isn't really bad, but he's got a quick temper and I imagine that whack on his sore arm hurt like blazes. You prevented him from doing something he would have been sorry for a moment later and which would very likely have landed him in serious trouble."

"So I judged and figured he'd better be stopped," Slade replied.

"You stopped him, all right," Beckley chuckled. "Blazes! what shooting! And I didn't miss that 'inside the gunhand', and neither did Chuck; he shivered."

"There is always an element of chance in any shooting," Slade smiled.

Beckley chuckled again. "And I've a notion that when you *miss,* the other fellow doesn't have much chance," he said meaningly.

"Just wanted you to know how I feel about it," he added. "The same goes for Chuck, even though now he's sorta clewed up both port and starboard, and for the other boys, too. Well, I guess I'd better round them up and head for home; work to do tomorrow. If you happen to be riding east, drop in at my place. About six miles out, the old gray casa in a grove of burr oaks; you can spot it from the trail."

With a smile and a nod he sauntered back to his men. A few minutes later they high-heeled out in a body. Chuck grinned and bobbed as he passed the table. The others also nodded.

Slade rolled another cigarette and thoughtfully regarded the swinging doors. He had arrived at two conclusions relative to Dick Beckley: he was a man of some education, and he had had something to do with the sea. Both of which *El Halcón* found interesting.

Puffing his cigarette, he pondered his next move, and arrived at a decision. It wasn't so very late and he felt restless. He'd get the rig on Shadow, pick up Marie at the cantina — he knew she had a horse stabled nearby — and they'd ride across the International Bridge and pay Nuevo Laredo a visit. He liked Nuevo Laredo, which was always warm and gay.

Just as he was preparing to put his plan into action, Amos Rolf, the purchasing agent, came in. He swept the room with his quick glance, waved to Slade and approached the bar. Ordering a drink, he downed it at a gulp, ordered another and consumed it almost as quickly. Then, with another wave of his hand, he hurried out. Was in a dickens of a rush for some reason, Slade thought. Well, he had plenty on his hands and doubtless scant time for loafing. A moment later, Slade waved goodnight to Gorty and also left the saloon, heading for the stable.

The thought of Nuevo Laredo brought something else to mind, something to which he had been giving considerable thought — the Indian Crossing.

The Indian Crossing, slightly north of the river end of Bruni Street, was a ledge of limestone rock lying just below the surface of the river, and in exceedingly dry seasons became partially exposed. It was known to the Indian tribes for centuries before the white men found it, and even later they used it to run cattle and horses, usually stolen from settlers, across the Rio Grande.

So after saddling up, Slade decided to ride down Bruni Street first and have a look at the Crossing. After which he could circle around and reach the cantina on Grant Street without undue delay.

There were no buildings close to the river, the street was deserted. There were a few clumps of trees and thickets on both sides of the street, which wasn't much of a street by the time it reached the river.

Where he had a good view of the swirl and eddy that marked the Crossing, which was now submerged, the river being rather high, he drew rein and sat contemplating the star dimpled water to the north of the Crossing. It was deep and comparatively calm, but on the downside it boiled and spouted furiously in tossing whirlpools.

"Bad down there," he remarked to the horse. "Would pound you to pieces in no time." He returned his gaze northward.

"Horse, I believe it would work," he said. "Always there is deep water to the north of the ledge, for no matter how low the river is, it has to rise enough on the up-side to flow over the ledge in places."

Suddenly Shadow pricked his ears forward and blew softly through his nose.

Slade knew what that meant and turned quickly to sweep the surrounding terrain with his gaze. Nothing met his eyes save the clumps of thicket, none of which were very close.

"Now what in blazes —" he began.

A shot rang out like a thunderclap in the

stillness. A slug whined past overhead. The sound seemed to come from a thicket close to the street and nearly directly behind him.

Almost instantly, another shot sounded from the left, still another from the right, the bullets whistling past uncomfortably close. He was surrounded, and neatly trapped. Did he ride back the way he came, or to the left, or to the right, he would be riding into gunfire. If he stayed where he was, one of the slugs would surely find its mark.

Slade's mind worked at racing speed. Only one alternative offered. It would be taking one devil of a chance, with the river as it was, but it was a chance, and there was certainly no other. He sent Shadow plunging forward onto the ledge.

The horse snorted protest but kept going, the water boiling around his hocks, his ankles, his knees. He reeled and staggered, fighting the mighty beat of the current, keeping his balance on the slippery stone by miracles of agility. Slade had used the Crossing before, but never with the river as high as it was at the present and not under such perilous circumstances.

The slugs were coming closer. Glancing back, he saw men running toward the river, shooting as they came. He slid his high-powered Winchester from the saddle boot and sprayed the river bank with bullets.

A yell echoed the reports, and a volley of curses. A slug fanned the Ranger's cheek with its lethal breath. Another ripped the crown of his hat. He emptied the magazine over his shoulder, slammed the rifle back into the boot and gave all his attention to riding. He abruptly realized no more lead was coming close. He had outdistanced six-gun range and, fortunately for him, it appeared the drygulchers had no rifles.

But just the same, his position was devilishly bad. They were near the middle of the river and the water was almost up to Shadow's barrel. The mighty rush of the current thrust and pounded against the great horse, threatening to any minute hurl him off his feet and doom horse and rider to death amid the whirlpools and rocks below. Once a hind foot skated over the lip and Slade thought they were gone. But with a lunge and a surge, Shadow recovered and staggered on, his breath whistling through his spreading nostrils, his eyes gorged with blood, on the verge of exhaustion.

Slade felt despair gripping his heart. The gallant animal had given his all, and it looked like it wasn't enough. Then with a surge of relief, he realized the water was shoaling. The whirlpools roared angrily and seemed to reach clutching fingers of foam and spray toward their intended victims. But now, with the pound of the current greatly lessened, Shadow was recovering, his superb strength flowing back into his veins. He tossed his head and snorted with triumph. He had done the impossible. To blazes with the darned old Rio Grande! It wasn't such-a-much! Three more minutes and he scrambled onto dry land, to stand for a moment with widespread front legs and hanging head. Slade stroked his neck and talked to him, his voice quivering a little with emotion. Shadow raised his head, shook himself and snorted as if to say,

"And now what, terrapin-brain? If you'd paid attention to what went on around you instead of moon-calfing with your head in the clouds, it wouldn't have happened."

With which his master perforce agreed.

"Well, we headed for Nuevo Laredo and we got here, though not exactly as planned," he said. "Now across the bridge and to the stable for you. I'll walk from there to the cantina."

Which he did, after giving Shadow a good rubdown and a generous helping of oats.

Marie greeted him gaily, but her eyes widened when she took a second look.

"What in heaven's name have you been up to?" she demanded. "You're all wet!"

Slade told her, without reservation. "You showed me the Crossing and how to use it when I was here before," he reminded her. "It came in handy then, and even handier tonight. Without it, my number would have been up."

Marie shook her curly head and sighed. "Maybe I'll get used to you and the things you do, some day, but I doubt it," she said. "I'll get some hot coffee . . . I've a notion you need it. Almost closing time."

9

The inquest over the two drygulchers was short, the verdict also short, declaring, in substance, that the sidewinders got just what was coming to them, belatedly.

After the inquest, Slade detailed the night before's misadventures for the benefit of Sheriff Medford, who swore luridly when the account was finished. Abruptly he asked a question,

"And Beckley and his hellions left the Montezuma before you did, eh?"

"They did," Slade replied.

"Well . . ."

"Don't jump at conclusions," Slade repeated his former warning. "There is absolutely no proof that the Triangle C bunch had anything to do with it."

"Maybe not," Medford growled, "but it all looks sorta funny to me. Another one of your coincidences, eh?"

"Could be," Slade admitted smilingly.

"By the way," he added, "did you locate the horses those two drygulchers rode?"

The sheriff shook his head.

"Not a hair of 'em," he replied. "We searched all the stables and racks. No unclaimed cayuses in the stables, no strays at the racks. Wonder what became of them?"

"Appears that some others of the bunch spirited them away," Slade guessed. "Looks like the brands might have told us something that somebody didn't want us to know."

"Or maybe those horned toads have been holed up in town and didn't have any broncs here," the sheriff hazarded.

"Possibly, but improbably," Slade answered, his black brows drawing together slightly.

He was thinking of another "coincidence" that quite likely meant nothing, but then again could possibly mean a good deal. And, as he told Medford, a Ranger cannot afford to overlook any leads, even those that, on the surface, appear ridiculous.

"Well, suppose we amble over to the Montezuma and grab off a bite to eat?" Medford suggested. "Inquests make me hungry."

Slade had no objections and they repaired to the restaurant. They were discussing the "bite" when a man entered who attracted

Slade's attention. He was tall and slender with raven-black hair and cool dark eyes. He was exceedingly handsome, his features almost cameo-like in their regularity. Although undoubtedly well past middle age the litheness of his stride and the spring of his step showed he had far from lost the fire and vigor of his youth.

"Fire" was aptly descriptive, Slade thought. The kind of fire that without warning explodes in dynamic action.

Medford noted the direction of the Ranger's gaze. "Everybody shows up at the Montezuma, sooner or later. That's why I hang out in here a lot," he said. "That's Rafael Gonzales, the head man of the ranchers over around Zapata who are quite a bit bothered about the validity of their titles, most of which date back to the grants of old Tomas Sanchez. *He's* sure got no use for the irrigation project, and he has a following."

Slade nodded soberly and regarded Gonzales. Things got more complicated all the time, with the hot Spanish blood of the Zapata residents to reckon with.

But what was the explanation of the whole loco business? Who was back of it, and why? Who could hope to profit by it, and how? Those were questions to which he must find the answers, and he had an uneasy feeling that time was growing short. There was no doubt but that the presence of *El Halcón* in the section was having a singularly disquieting effect on somebody. Witness, the frantic efforts to eliminate him. And Slade felt they approached the frantic. The try the night before had been handled more skillfully than the crude attempt from the alley across from Miguel's cantina. The same might be said of the hydraulic giant's nozzleman.

"But Shadow was right last night," he told himself. "I was careless and not paying proper attention to what went on around me. Those hellions must have been watching the Montezuma, expecting that sooner or later I would show, and tailed me to the river. Very likely, I'd say, by way of Poggenpohl Street, which parallels Bruni on the north, then they cut across and holed up in the thickets. Darn lucky for me those clumps of brush weren't closer, or they might have gotten away with it. As it was, they doubtless figured they had me right where they wanted, either not counting on the Indian Crossing, or figuring that only a stark staring lunatic would attempt the ledge with the river high as it is. Well, if it hadn't been for Shadow, they would have been right. The average horse would never have made it.

"Looks to be a capable individual," he observed to Medford.

"Not a bad sort, Gonzales," replied the sheriff. "Always pleasant to everybody, unless something riles him. Has the courtesy of the real oldtimer of pure Spanish blood. Expect he'll drop over to speak to me before he leaves; always does. He's an educated feller, and I think you'd like him."

"Quite probably," Slade conceded.

The sheriff speculated Gonzales. "Looks to be in a bad temper over something right now," he observed.

Slade thought so, too. The rancher was glowering moodily at the backbar and toying with his drink. From time to time his lips moved slightly, as if he were muttering to himself. Once he shook his shapely head in an exasperated manner.

"Yes, something's got him on the prod," the Ranger remarked.

"Something to do with the irrigation project, you can bet on that. Just wait and see."

The sheriff was to prove himself a prophet with honor, even in his own county.

Gonzales abruptly downed his drink, turned and walked to the table.

"Howdy, Rafe!" the sheriff greeted. "Take

a load off your feet. I want you and Walt Slade to know each other."

Gonzales had a pleasant smile and his eyes warmed as he shook hands.

"Have heard quite a bit about you, Mr. Slade," he said. "It is a pleasure to meet up with you."

"What you pawin' sod about, Rafe?" the sheriff asked, after ordering drinks.

"You know what," Gonzales replied. "Those blasted irrigation people. Looks like I've a very good chance to lose my holding, but not without a fight, not without a fight."

"Fight it out in the courts," the sheriff advised. "You have your copy of the grant, haven't you?"

"I have not," Gonzales stated. "That occurred in my great-grandfather's time. I haven't the slightest notion what became of the papers, after all those years. Never gave it any thought before, and who in blazes would have thought the title would ever be questioned. The property has been in my family for generations."

Slade spoke. "Mr. Gonzales, do you have a definite knowledge that your title is going to be questioned?" he asked.

"Why . . . why no," Gonzales admitted. "But I understand that it is."

"Has anyone with authority to do so told

you that your title will be questioned?" Slade persisted. Gonzales hesitated, then shook his head.

"But the word is going around that all our titles based on the old grant will be challenged," he replied defensively.

"Then you admit that your contention is based on hearsay?"

"Well, now . . ." Gonzales began, but Slade interrupted, his gaze hard on the other's face.

"Have the irrigation people notified you that your title is to be questioned?"

Gonzales again shook his head.

"Has the Land Office notified you that the validity of your title is to be challenged?"

For the third time, Gonzales had to shake his head.

"Then," Slade said, his voice hardening, "you are getting on your high horse over nothing more substantial than vague gossip, isn't that right? Do you consider your position exactly tenable?"

Gonzales flushed. Then suddenly he smiled.

"Mr. Slade," he said, "just what are you getting at?"

"Just this," Slade replied. "You have been tilting at windmills, to employ an expression, getting all riled up over a chimera. My advice to you is to wait until somebody with the authority to do so does in a legal manner question your title, which in my opinion will never happen."

Gonzales looked a trifle bewildered, but relieved. "Mr. Slade," he said, "you've made me feel one devil of a sight better." He added diffidently, "I'd sorta like to shake hands again."

They did so, and Gonzales' clasp was warm.

"But what's the meaning of those rumors that have been going around?" he asked. "Why are they going around?"

"It means, in my opinion, that somebody is deliberately endeavoring to stir up trouble between the irrigation people and the ranch owners," Slade replied grimly. "Why? At the moment I don't know, but I hope to learn, and who started them."

"Mr. Slade," Gonzales said deliberately, "in *my* opinion, you will learn, and somebody won't enjoy the learning."

"Rafe, you can say that double," chuckled the sheriff.

Gonzales insisted on buying another round of drinks. After which he stood up.

"I rode in to have a talk with my lawyer," he said. "Don't figure I need to. I'm going over to the hotel and sign for a room; don't feel like another forty-miles ride today. Hope to see you later, Mr. Slade, and you, too, Tobe."

"Well," said the sheriff as they watched his tall form pass through the swinging doors, "well, I've a notion you plumb dried up one source of trouble. He was all set to hit back. He's an impetuous sort, and so are the rest of his crowd. Any little thing would have set them off. Now I don't think we need to worry."

"Perhaps not where Gonzales is concerned," Slade conceded. "But we've still got plenty to worry about. I seem to be getting exactly nowhere."

"You'll get somewhere, and fast," the sheriff predicted cheerfully. "No doubt in my mind as to that. Let us drink!"

"I think I winged one of those hellions last night, although not seriously," Slade remarked.

"And I'll be keeping my eyes skun for another horned toad with his arm in a sling," Medford said meaningly.

Slade refrained from comment.

The afternoon was moving along. The sheriff moseyed out to look things over. Slade ordered another cup of coffee, rolled a cigarette and gave himself over to thought. He felt he had plenty to think about, and at the moment his cogitations were not satisfactory or productive of satisfactory results.

Finally, he gave it up; he'd try the open air for a spell, he could always think best in the open air. Perhaps walk down Bruni Street to the river. He was on the verge of departing when Sheriff Medford reappeared, in a hurry, and flopped into a chair.

"Was afraid I'd miss you," he said. "Got something to tell you." He gazed at the Ranger and shook his head.

"I don't know how you do it! I don't know how you do it!" he declared. "I never heard of such a persuasive voice as you have. When you sing, rattlesnakes and horned toads shed tears. When you talk, soft and low, to a feller who's all riled up and bothered like Gonzales was, you send him away smiling and with his head up."

"Yes?" Slade prompted smilingly, for he knew the foregoing was a preamble to imparting information.

"I met Gonzales coming out of the hotel," the sheriff explained. "We stopped to talk. Along came Clark, the engineer for the irrigation project. I know him and he sorta slowed up to say hello. Well, Gonzales walked right up to him. 'Mr. Clark,' he said, 'I owe you an apology. I've been saying some rather mean things about you people, but it appears I have been very much in the wrong. I hope you will forget what is past.' "

The sheriff paused, and drew a deep breath. "And," he concluded sententiously, "they shook hands and went off to have a drink together. I don't know how you do it!"

"Perhaps the answer is that people who are bothered with problems are too close to them; they obscure all else. Let someone distract their thoughts, as it were, from the immediate problem and all of a sudden they obtain a clearer view and broader understanding which enable them to acquire an unclouded perspective," was Slade's answer.

"I suppose so, whatever the devil that means," sighed the sheriff. "Well, be seeing you later. I sorta got detracked on my way to the office. Thought you'd like to hear about what happened."

"I did," Slade replied, "and I'm very pleased about it."

Later, Slade was to ponder the importance of seemingly inconsequential things. Had the sheriff not delayed his departure for a few minutes, he, Slade, would have very likely sauntered down Bruni Street instead of turning his steps down Juarez Street to

Farragut Street and the Mexican Railroad station.

He was nearing the station when he saw, on a siding, locomotive and caboose attached, a green and gold splendor with "Winona" stenciled on the side. It was the private car of General Manager James G. "Jaggers" Dunn of the great C. & P. Railroad System. He whistled under his breath, for at the moment there was no man in the world he would rather have seen than Jaggers Dunn. He quickened his stride and mounted the steps of the coach and shoved open the door.

Sam, the G.M.'s porter, chef, and general factotum was pottering about. He let out a whoop of greeting.

"Boss Man, Boss Man!" he called. "Look who's here!

Jaggers himself came rumbling into the drawing room and added his own stentorian greeting.

"Walt! Where the devil did you come from? I'm sure glad you happened along right when you did. We're pulling out in an hour for Mexico. You know I'm sorta interested in the Mexican Railroad and want to gather a little firsthand information. Hey! do I sniff gunpowder? Must be trouble in the wind with you here. Never knew it to fail."

"Well, I'm afraid there is," Slade replied as he shook hands with Dunn and the porter.

"Sam," ordered Jaggers, "break out a bottle and fix a snack and put coffee on to heat. Sit down, Walt, and tell me about it."

Slade proceeded to do so, in detail. Dunn listened in silence, now and then passing his hand over the glorious crinkly white mane that swept back from his big dome-shaped forehead, a habit with him when he was deeply interested.

"Mr. Dunn," Slade concluded, "what do you know of the people who are handling the irrigation project here?"

"They're okay, square-shooters," Dunn instantly responded. "What they have in mind will confer a great benefit on the section, if they are successful. So somebody is making trouble for them, eh? That's not good. They are solvent, but their resources are not unlimited and very likely their backers are getting a bit nervous."

"That's what I'm afraid," Slade replied. "Do you have any notion who might be interested in delaying or thwarting the project?"

Dunn was silent a moment, then . . .

"Walt," he asked, "did you ever hear of

109

the Neches Waterway promoters?"

"Why, yes," Slade replied. "That was the bunch that froze out Oliver Stilton and took over his Port Arthur holdings, were they not?"

"That's right," nodded Dunn. "A predatory outfit that will stop at nothing to achieve their ends. Ethics to them is just a word in the dictionary. So far they've always gotten by, usually leaving somebody else holding the bag, I have heard they have an eye on this project. If they should happen to gain control, it would be very much to the detriment of the people who plan to buy and settle here."

"I see," Slade said slowly.

"And you may also see," Jaggers countered, "that you are all of a sudden in the middle of a fight between giants."

"Yes," Slade admitted, "but in such a business there are always key men who direct and carry out operations. Eliminate them and you are well on the way to solving your problem."

"You'll do it, all right," Dunn predicted. "That is if you manage to stay alive, which, under the circumstances, looks to be something of a chore."

"I'm alive now, and that's all that counts," Slade answered lightly.

"Oh, I figure you'll get by," Dunn retorted. "As I've said before, I figure some particular devil accompanies you who looks after his own."

"Not a bad sort of devil to have around," Slade smiled. Jaggers snorted and said some things that smelled of sulphur.

Over the snack and the coffee they talked until it was time for the one-car train to pull out for Mexico. Dunn and Sam waved goodbye from the back platform. Slade headed toward Grant Street in a pleased frame of mind. He figured he had learned a good deal. Now, at least, he knew what he was up against, and being familiar with the methods employed by the Neches Waterway bunch, he felt better able to cope with them.

He was convinced the information he had gathered was authentic; there was very little going on in the financial world that Jaggers Dunn didn't know about.

Slade did not underestimate his opponents; he had already had ample proof that they would stop at nothing. Shrewd, ruthless, with great resources, they were accustomed to winning and to brush aside all opposition, no matter who got hurt in the course of the brushing. He had a chore confronting him, calculated to give even *El Halcón* pause.

However, he was forced to admit, albeit a trifle guiltily, that he actually looked forward to the coming conflict not with apprehension but with complacent anticipation; it was good to do battle with such forces, from the viewpoint of a Texas Ranger. Which was one of the reasons he *was* a Texas Ranger.

10

As he entered the cantina, Slade was surprised to see, at a table against the far wall, three familiar faces. One was Clark, the irrigation engineer, the second was Rafael Gonzales, the third, Amos Rolf, the purchasing agent.

The trio were so engrossed in their talk that they did not note his entrance. Being in no mood for conversation, he quietly made his way to a small table back of a corner of the dance floor and ordered coffee.

Regarding the scene of amicable relations at the far table, Slade experienced a pleasurable glow. Gonzales, the acknowledged leader of the Zapata ranchers, would undoubtedly swing the descendants of the hot-blooded Spaniards into line. Slade felt he had accomplished something that would quite likely simplify his own problem.

That the force arrayed against him would

strike back in some fashion was a foregone conclusion, something he must guard against; but he felt that each move against him, so long as it was not successful, left his antagonists just a little more vulnerable, there always being the element of chance that the move would be fumbled, which would work to his advantage, even to possibly giving him a lead on the "higher-up" who was directing operations.

What the next move might be he had no idea, but was convinced it would be something subtle and well planned, perhaps carried out in an indirect manner. It was quite probable that his adversaries had, as others before them, arrived at the conclusion that trying to drygulch *El Halcón* was a highly dangerous business and just a waste of time.

When the move was made, it was unexpected, in the nature of a surprise, and very nearly caught *El Halcón* flat-footed. But it did give him something to work on, a vague and inconclusive lead, but a lead.

While Slade was discussing his coffee, Amos Rolf said a few final words to his companions and left the cantina. If he saw Slade sitting in his corner, he gave no indication of the fact. Clark and Gonzales remained at the table, talking.

A little later, however, they also departed.

Slade, wishing to be alone with his thoughts, did nothing to attract their attention.

Glancing at the clock, he wondered why Marie had not yet put in an appearance, for it was already growing dark and the cantina becoming busy; he couldn't imagine what was holding her.

When she did appear, not long afterward, he got a surprise, a pleasant one. Accompanying her was a tall, laughing-eyed girl and a slender, wiry young Mexican with alert black eyes and a face that was usually absolutely expressionless. Now, however, the eyes grew warm and the somber face was brightened by a white smile as he approached Slade. The pair were Rosa, Marie's sister, and her husband, Estaban Fuentes.

"I sent them word that you were here and of course they hurried to town to greet you," Marie said. "Don't they look wonderful?"

"They sure do," Slade replied. "Ranching agrees with them."

"And isn't Marie radiant!" Rosa exclaimed. "She looks just like a bride. That is, a bride of a year or so."

"Rosa, you are impossible!" Marie said, blushing hotly.

"Am I?" Rosa returned innocently. "Estaban thinks I'm wonderful. Of course, he hasn't must choice . . . he's stuck with me. And he's always around to keep an eye on me. That's the advantage of having a . . . er . . . husband who gallivants off ever so often. When he does show up it's like a second honeymoon. And you look wonderful, too, Walt. Oh, well, I guess you needed a rest, and profited from it."

"*Will* you stop talking and sit down and have a drink!" Marie cut in exasperatedly.

"And something to eat," added Rosa. "I'm starved, as usual. Here come the dance floor girls. Aren't they beautiful? How could any man resist them! Estaban! keep your eyes this way!"

Marie had not changed to her dance costume. Slade glanced at her street dress. She interpreted his glance.

"I'm off tonight," she explained. "Nothing to do all night."

"Hmmm!" said Rosa.

They had a very pleasant dinner together. Miguel brought over a bottle of his own favorite wine. After eating they danced several numbers.

Rosa made a suggestion. "How about crossing the river to Nuevo Laredo?" she said. "I haven't been there for quite a while."

"And we'll walk," said Marie, jumping to her feet.

Nobody objected, so they set out, strolling down Convent Avenue and crossing the river by way of the International Foot Bridge and reaching Nuevo Laredo, gay, lively, colorful.

Everywhere there was music, drifting over the doors of the cantinas, arising from the guitars and voices of the wandering troubadours in their charro costumes, including gay sombreros, embroidered serapes and velvet pantaloons, always the center of a throng.

Before the door of a softly lighted cantina, Marie paused. "You remember this place, don't you, Walt?" she said. "It is where you met Ralpho Flores the bandit leader, known as *El Cascabel,* The Rattlesnake."

"Yes," Slade replied, recalling the grim and tragic happenings, including the death of Flores and Wilton Danver, the head of the notorious Land Committee.

"Shall we go in?" asked Marie.

"Why not?" Slade replied.

They entered the cantina and found a table. Felipe, the owner, remembered Slade and greeted him warmly.

"We must drink," he said. "Of the wine that only Felipe and his *amigos* drink." He hurried to fetch a bottle.

After doing justice to the golden wine, Estaban left for a little while to visit a friend farther down the street. Slade and the girls danced a couple more numbers. They had just returned to the table when a familiar figure entered. Slade instantly recognized Rafael Gonzales, the Zapata rancher, who joined Felipe at the far end of the bar. Almost on his heels, Estaban returned. As he sat down, he jerked his head toward Gonzales.

"Know him, Walt?" he asked.

"Yes, I met him today," Slade replied. "Not a bad sort."

"He's okay," said Estaban. "A big man over at Zapata. Owns the best spread there and is head man of the ranchers. He and Felipe are friends and he often visits here. I noticed he had his bodyguard with him tonight, as usual."

"His bodyguard?"

"Yes," nodded Estaban. "A couple of his hands almost always ride to town with him and keep tabs on him, especially since he has had trouble with the irrigation people."

"I'm sure he told me he rode in alone today," Slade remarked.

Estaban shrugged. "As to that I know not," he answered in his precise Mission-taught English. "I only know that two men in rangeland clothes followed him closely along the crowded street and watched his every move. They did not enter the cantina, which surprised me, but doubtless they know their business."

"Yes, doubtless they do," Slade said with a grim significance that was lost on Estaban.

While taking part in the general conversation, Slade kept a close watch on Gonzales. He was sure the rancher had not noticed him, otherwise he would have most likely spoken or approached the table.

Gonzales' stay was brief. After a drink and a few words with Felipe, he headed for the swinging doors. Slade stood up.

"Stay where you are," he told his companions. "I'll be back soon."

Before they could protest or ask questions, he was gone.

Outside, he quickly spotted the tall form of the Zapata rancher. And almost as quickly he spotted the two men in cowhand clothes who trailed along behind him. Slade followed, not too closely, but close enough.

Gonzales walked purposefully, evidently heading for the bridge. As they neared the approach, the lighting grew poorer, with fewer pedestrians on the street. By the time they reached it, the street was deserted. Slade closed the distance a little. The two men, intent on their quarry, never turned to glance back.

Suddenly they darted forward. Slade saw the gleam of an upraised knife. He drew and shot, and again the knife spun through the air. There was a howl of pain. The descending hand struck Gonzales on the side of the head and knocked him sprawling. The two men whirled about to face *El Halcón* and the deserted street fairly exploded to a bellow of gunfire.

Seconds later, Walt Slade, two holes in his shirt sleeve, blood trickling from a bullet graze along his left temple, lowered his smoking Colts, glanced at the two figures slumped on the ground and rushed to assist Gonzales to rise.

"Come on, don't stop to ask questions," he said, gripping the rancher by the arm and hauling him to his feet, half dazed by the blow.

"This way, *Capitan,*" a voice called behind them. It was Estaban, who had *not* stayed "where he was."

Following the young Mexican's lead, they circled about and approached the lighted streets by a devious route. By which time Gonzales had completely recovered.

"Mr. Slade," he panted, for the going had been fast, "Mr. Slade, you undoubtedly

120

saved my life, which I will not forget, but why did those men seek to kill me?"

"If you had been killed, what would your neighbors, the other Zapata ranchers have thought and who would they have blamed?" Slade answered.

"Why — why I suppose they would have blamed the irrigation people," Gonzales replied.

"Exactly," Slade said. "Somebody was very anxious that you did not return to them with the word that you had patched up your differences with the irrigation people, knowing that the other ranchers, your friends, would follow your lead. Remember, I told you that somebody was deliberately endeavoring to stir up trouble in the section. Beginning to understand?"

"Yes, I think I am," Gonzales said slowly. He shuddered. "I was near death tonight," he added. "Thank you again, Mr. Slade. And who is your fine friend here?"

Estaban was introduced and they paused long enough to shake hands.

"Now back to the cantina," Slade said. "You are staying with us the rest of the night, Mr. Gonzales, and we will cross the bridge together."

"And I will feel as safe as were I a babe in my mother's arms," Gonzales declared with conviction.

"Ha!" Estaban suddenly chuckled. "Folks will do much puzzling over the bodies of those *ladrones.* Well, what they do not know will hurt them not."

"Yes, we got in the clear before somebody came to investigate the shooting," Slade said. "Which was what I wished to do; the less questions to answer the better. And I think some people will do quite a bit of puzzling," he added cryptically.

"What I can't understand," said Gonzales, "is how somebody learned I had changed my mind relative to the irrigation people. I mentioned it only to Mr. Clark and Mr. Rolf."

"Sometimes the wrong pair of ears overhears what is said," Slade replied without further comment.

But his eyes were cold as frosted steel as he spoke.

"I am sure that tonight a friend arrived with a couple of his hands," continued Gonzales. "He planned to pause briefly at the Bar A ranch a few miles east of town. Tomorrow, I will contact him and ride to Zapata in his company."

"A good notion," Slade agreed. "I don't think you have anything more to worry about, but best not to take chances. Once you reach the Zapata section and your neighbors there, the hellions will lose interest in you."

"I hope so," sighed Gonzales. "It is not good to have enemies of such nature."

When they arrived at the cantina, they found the girls decidedly nervous. Marie instantly spotted the smear of blood on Slade's forehead.

"I knew it!" she exclaimed, dabbing at the slight skin cut with a wisp of lacy handkerchief. "Let you out of my sight for five minutes and you're in trouble. All right, tell us about it."

Slade told them, briefly. Gonzales was introduced and added some comments relative to the part Slade played.

"Mr. Slade saved my life," he concluded. "I will not forget. Tell me, Mr. Slade," he added, "was it accident that your bullet struck that knife and the hand that wielded it?"

Estaban gave a sardonic chuckle. "Is it accident when the falcon makes its swoop?"

11

It was late when they left the cantina, but they crossed the bridge without incident. Leaving the girls at Marie's cottage on Matamoros Street, Slade and Estaban accompanied Gonzales to the hotel and saw him safe inside his room.

The following afternoon, Slade and Sheriff Medford rode to Nuevo Laredo and visited the mayor.

"Heard you had a shooting here last night, Juan," said the sheriff.

"That's right," replied the *alcalde.* "Two hard looking *ladrones* were found by the bridge approach. We presume they shot each other. The bodies are at the undertaker's. Would you like to see them?"

"Yes, I would," said Medford. "We had a couple of killings in our town the other night. I'm sorta curious if I happen to know the pair you corralled."

However, after viewing the bodies, the

sheriff shook his head. "Never saw either of 'em before," he admitted. "Ornery lookin' scuts."

As they retrieved their horses, he turned to Slade. "Did you spot anything?" he asked.

"Only that they had black river-bottom mud on their boots," the Ranger replied.

"Meaning?"

"Meaning, as a guess, that they spent some time around the irrigation project."

A little later, Slade took another ride, to the site of the irrigation project, where everything was bustling activity. The hydraulic giant was not operating at the moment and he saw nothing of the errant nozzleman. Nor was Amos Rolf in evidence.

Once again *El Halcón* studied the inlet lead channels and arrived at the same conclusion as on his former visit. After a bit he contacted Ernest Clark, the engineer in charge of the project, who greeted him cordially.

"Mr. Clark," he asked, after a few minutes of casual conversation, "are you familiar with the vagaries of this river?"

"Why, not particularly," Clark admitted. "However, Mr. Rolf is. Why?"

Slade ignored the question. "Mr. Clark," he said, "suppose after the project is completed it is found that your inlet channels

125

are not deep enough, the gradient too slight, so that in times when the river is very low, which often obtains for an extensive period, you cannot get any water to replenish your impoundings, what would be the effect on your reputation as an engineer?"

"Why . . . why," replied the startled Clark, "it would be ruinous."

Slade let the full force of his steady eyes rest on the engineer's face.

"Mr. Clark," he said deliberately, "unless your inlet lead channels are deepened by at least a dozen feet and the gradient increased by around nine per cent, that is exactly what is going to happen." He held up his hand as the engineer started to protest.

"Mr. Clark," he pursued, "without mentioning what I just told you to anyone, I mean *anyone,* check with the Reclamation Service on the mean rise and fall of the river at this point and see if I am not right."

Now Clark was decidedly worried. "Mr. Slade," he said, "I'll do it, without delay."

"You can do so by telegraph," Slade told him. "And I repeat, please do not mention this conversation to anyone; I have my reasons for requesting that you do not."

"I won't," Clark promised. He shot the Ranger a curious glance.

"You are an engineer, Mr. Slade?" he asked.

"I know something of the principles of engineering," Slade replied with a smile.

"Something!" Clark repeated dryly. "Yes, I've a notion you do. Thank you, Mr. Slade, for what you told me." He grinned boyishly. "I hope you're plumb wrong," he added, "but blast it! I've a very unpleasant feeling that you are not. I'll do as you said, at once, and I won't talk."

"Thank you," Slade said, and they shook hands.

Walt Slade rode back to town quite pleased with the afternoon's work. He knew perfectly well what the report of the Reclamation Service was going to be.

"But, Shadow," he remarked to the horse, "how in blazes did the hellion get away with it? He must have a lot of folks hypnotized including Clark."

Shadow did not appear impressed, and his answering snort was noncommittal.

After stabling the big black, Slade entered the Montezuma for coffee and expected to contact Sheriff Medford a little later. He rolled a cigarette and conned over the happenings of the past twenty-four hours. The summing up was quite satisfactory, so far as it went. He had cemented the friendship of

127

Rafael Gonzales and had strengthened his resolve to persuade his followers to refrain from further antagonism toward the irrigation project. He had done something to advance the project. And he believed he had finally, to an extent at least, narrowed his list of potential suspects.

Also, the motive was now fairly clear. The motivating force . . . greed. Quite often the motivating force in such an affair, one way or another. And all too often accompanied by utter ruthlessness, as in this case. Well, with somebody to keep an eye on, at last, the problem was somewhat clarified, the solution more definite.

How to arrive at the solution he had not at the moment the slightest idea. Suspecting was one thing, proving another, and so far he had absolutely no proof against any suspect. He could only let events take their course and hope to turn them to his advantage. Perhaps something would react favorably, something usually did.

With which, he proceeded to enjoy his coffee and cigarette with a free mind.

Shortly afterward, Sheriff Medford arrived. "Well, Gonzales is on his way home with one of his rancher *amigos* and four cowhands for company," he announced. "Guess he should make out."

"Yes, doubtless he will," Slade agreed. "Once he arrives at Zapata he is safe; no longer anything to be gained by doing him harm."

"You sure took him in tow," chuckled the sheriff. "He couldn't talk about anything else. His rancher friend sorta mentioned he's heard some folks say you were an owlhoot. Gonzales hit the ceiling. I thought he was going to throw some punches. The other feller backed water in a hurry.

"Well, it ain't surprising, the way he feels. I've a notion he sorta likes being alive."

"A fairly normal reaction," Slade smiled.

"Yep, I guess that's so," the sheriff conceded. "Well, I'm going to try to hit the hay early. Quiet tonight but it won't be tomorrow night. Tomorrow is payday for the irrigation workers and the spreads hereabouts. Tomorrow night Laredo will howl. What you plan to do?"

"I'm going down to Miguel's place and then try to emulate your example," Slade replied. "Be seeing you."

The next afternoon, Slade again rode to the irrigation project. There he found the dirt flying. The channels were being deepened, the gradient changed. Clark hurried forward with outstretched hand, his face wreathed in smiles.

"You were absolutely right," he said. "The Reclamation people agreed with you in every detail. You sure saved my bacon, and my company a lot of money. I told Mr. Rolf what I planned to do, of course not mentioning our conversation, and he concurred wholeheartedly and congratulated me on discovering the error. I felt ashamed, listening to his praise and knowing I had no right to take credit."

"I prefer it that way," Slade said.

"And of course I have to defer to your wishes," answered Clark. His eyes grew reflective.

"Mr. Rolf doesn't often make mistakes," he remarked with apparent irrelevance.

"So I would judge," Slade agreed.

"Well, I'm letting the boys knock off a bit early to make ready for their payday bust . . . they've earned it," said Clark. "And they don't have to report for work until noon tomorrow. I suppose some of them will show up with blue eyes and busted noses, but they're a hardy lot and can usually look out for themselves.

"I figure I'm due a mite of celebrating myself," he added with his boyish grin. "Yes, I think I am, thanks to you. I suppose you'll be in the Montezuma tonight? Fine! I hope to run into you and we'll have a drink together."

As he rode slowly back to town through the dusk, Slade remarked to Shadow . . .

"Well, horse, we're up against a shrewd and resourceful proposition. Lots of folks can take a winning in stride, but few can take defeat without turning a hair. To him the loss of a skirmish is just an incentive to double his efforts. We haven't heard the last of this little episode, on that you can wager your last helping of oats. He'll strike back, and he'll strike hard. We've got to really be on our toes from now on. Won't do to make a mistake; liable to be our last one."

"Speak for yourself, John," the toss of Shadow's head seemed to reply. "I'm not in the habit of making mistakes. That is unless it was taking up with you. As to that I sometimes wonder a mite."

Slade chuckled and tweaked his ears, and was rewarded for his temerity with a snap of milk-white teeth that barely missed their mark, and wouldn't have missed had Shadow really meant it.

"Now if I can just put across my other little scheme, this one that has to do with the Indian Cross, I've a notion *amigo* Clark will get a raise in salary," Slade added as they neared the stable. "That will require considerable conniving, however. I still can't

help wondering why somebody hasn't already hit on it. Plain as the nose on your
face, which is plenty plain. Perhaps somebody has, not the right somebody, of course.
Wouldn't put it past the hellion. How in the
devil does he get by with what he does and
still stay in the background? Sure wish I'd
hit on my lead before old Jim Dunn headed
into Mexico. Well, he should be back any
day now and we'll see him. Perhaps he can
give us a hand; I've a notion he can."

After making sure all Shadow's wants
were properly provided against, Slade
headed for Miguel's cantina. Very quickly
he was of the opinion that the sheriff's
prophecy of a wild night for Laredo was well
founded. Already cowhands were riding into
town, with plenty more on the way. Soon
they would be augmented by the irrigation
workers. Yes, Laredo was due to howl.
Slade's pulses quickened and he experienced a surge of anticipation.

For, young and filled with lusty life, he
had to admit that he liked such nights. And
he determined that for a while he would
forget his problems, throw himself into the
spirit of things and really enjoy himself.

Marie, gay, laughing, elfinly beautiful in
her abbreviated dance costume, strengthened his resolve; they'd make a night of it

132

together. She would be working on the floor, of course, but they'd manage to steal some time for themselves.

Miguel, his face beaming, came rolling across to greet Slade, under his arm, as usual, a bottle of rare vintage.

"Oh! to be young again!" he exclaimed, smiling from one to the other.

"Mike, you're younger than either one of us, and getting younger by the minute, and you might as well admit it," Slade told him.

"Ha! but my creaking joints and my palsied hands say different," Miguel replied, capering a dance step or two and raising a brimming glass without spilling a drop to prove his point. "Let us drink!"

They did so, laughing together. Miguel hurried back to the bar, which was already crowded. Marie ordered dinner. The cook stuck his head out the kitchen door, waved his hand and hurried back to outdo himself in deference to *El Halcón,* the honored guest.

"Everybody thinks you're wonderful," Marie said.

"Well, am I not?" he countered, falling in with her mood.

"Darn it! Haven't I told you often enough?" she retorted, the dimple showing at the corner of her vividly red mouth.

They ate their dinner with the appetite of

youth and perfect health and lingered over final cups of fragrant coffee.

After the cups were empty, Marie glanced at the crowded dance floor.

"Guess I'll have to get to work," she said. "Seems everybody wants to dance tonight and there aren't enough girls to go around. You're not running off somewhere?"

"Not for a while at least," he replied. "Later I may walk up to the Montezuma for a word with Sheriff Medford; I imagine he'll be hanging around there a good part of the night. But I'll be back soon."

"You'd better be," she warned. "Or I'll very likely dance off with some handsome *vaquero* and forget all about you . . . for a while."

Slade tried to look worried, and failed signally. Marie made a face at him and whisked off to the dance floor. Slade rolled a cigarette, settled back comfortably in his chair and surveyed the colorful scene.

12

Although the coming of the railroads had put an end to Laredo's isolation, it was still very much of a wild frontier town, and the payday bust in what was as yet predominantly cattleland was no tame affair. So far the crowd was boisterous but well behaved. Could well be different once the redeye began really getting in its licks. Even Miguel's place, which was usually noted for moderation, packed plenty of potential dynamite. And in this part of the world most anything could happen, and usually did.

It was a polyglot gathering. Lithe young *vaqueros* from across the river, clad in velvet adorned with much silver, rubbed shoulders with sinewy cowhands from the Texas spreads. There were bulky river front workers, and brawny irrigation men. Local shopkeepers and office workers, in store clothes, their more sober attire providing a balance for the kaleidoscope of color. The spangled costumes of the dance floor girls caught the light, and their laughing eyes reflected it, sometimes decidedly detrimental to the peace of mind of their partners, who missed steps in consequence.

Not that anybody cared, for stumbling provided an excuse for holding the girls tighter. Slade chuckled, and rolled another cigarette.

Marie, breathless and rosy, left the floor and joined him.

"I'm sitting this one out," she said. "I need a rest. The dance floor is a mad house. But I like it. Oh, by the way, I forgot to tell you Rosa and Estaban are coming . . . they stayed over for the payday celebration. They'll be late, though; stopped to visit with some friends.

"Now you're going to catch it," she suddenly added. "Here comes Navarro, the orchestra leader, with a guitar."

The ponderous leader approached the table, bowing and smiling.

"*Capitan* will sing?" he urged insinuatingly. "Please, *Capitan*."

"Okay, if the folks don't object," Slade acceded.

"They will not object," Navarro replied pleasantly, caressing the handle of the long knife that was part of his charro costume. He handed Slade the guitar and led the way to the *platforma* which accommodated the orchestra, and held up his hand.

Navarro also had a voice, not a singing voice. It was more like that of one of the bulls that fed on his father's pastures. By sheer bellowing he got silence, or very near it. His stentorian tones rang through the room:

"*Senoritas* and *senores,* I have for you the great treat. *Capitan* will sing!"

The crowd gazed expectantly at the tall form of *El Halcón.* Those who knew the truth nudged neighbors to keep them quiet. Slade smiled, threw back his black head and sang, first a rollicking ballad of the range.

And as his great metallic baritone-bass filled the room with melody, there was a hush such as not all Navarro's roaring could achieve. A hush that was a greater tribute to the singer than the storm of applause that followed, and the shouts for another.

Smiling his appreciation, Slade sang them another, and yet another. Concluding with a wistful and poignantly beautiful love song of his own composition, during which even hardened oldtimers passed furtive hands across their eyes and muttered something about the blasted smoke. While the dance floor girls didn't bother to brush the tears away.

With another smile, Slade returned the guitar to its owner. Navarro bowed low and murmured his thanks.

"Viva El Halcón!" somebody shouted. And the cheer was given with a will.

"The things you do to me when you sing!" Marie sighed as he rejoined her at the table.

"Only when I sing?"

"Shut up!" she retorted. "I'm going back on the floor." Which she proceeded to do. Slade rolled another cigarette and ordered more coffee. He felt comfortable and relaxed.

Gradually, however, he began to grow restless and wondered what the other places were like. Abruptly he recalled he had half-promised Clark, the irrigation engineer, to meet him in the Montezuma and decided to do so. Would also like a word with Sheriff Medford, who would in all probability show there sooner or later. Waving to Marie, he sauntered out.

Her eyes, darkening, followed him to the swinging doors and her answers to her dancing partner's sallies were distraught, although he *was* a handsome young *vaquero* with a charming presence and courtly manners.

Outside, Slade found the streets crowded and noisy, which was not strange; there were fully a hundred cowhands in town and perhaps twice that number of irrigation workers, to say nothing of town folk and visitors from Nuevo Laredo.

Arriving at the Montezuma without incident, he spotted Clark conversing with several of his foremen. Also present was Beckley, the Triangle C owner, with him Chuck Perkins, the cowhand, who no longer had his arm in a sling, along with several other Triangle C hands. They shouted a greeting.

Slade shook his head to the proffer of a drink; he had drunk a good deal of Miguel's special vintage wine and felt it was best to keep his mind clear and observant.

The small table at the corner of the dance floor was vacant, so he sat down and ordered coffee. A little later, Beckley sauntered over to the table.

"Mind if I join you for a few minutes?" he asked.

"Not at all," Slade replied. "Pull up a chair." He motioned to a waiter to bring drinks.

At that moment Gorty approached Ernest Clark and said something to him. Clark turned, glanced toward Slade and waved his hand. Slade instantly beckoned him. Clark hesitated, then crossed the room.

"Take a load off your feet," Slade invited, pulling out another chair, and ordering another drink.

Clark did so, hesitantly. He and Beckley regarded each other somewhat askance.

Suddenly Slade laughed merrily, his eyes crinkling at the corners, the little devils of mirth turning somersaults to the front.

"What's so darn funny?" Beckley asked in injured tones. Slade smiled broadly.

"I was thinking," he said, "of two strange dogs turning a corner and coming face to face to stand with their hackles rising and wondering, 'What the devil shall I do now?' "

His hearers "got" the implication and both grinned sheepishly.

"Mr. Beckley, Mr. Clark," *El Halcón* said, "Don't you think it is just a bit silly for two grown men to get their hackles up over what is fundamentally a business matter? As I understand it, Mr. Beckley claims a certain strip of land; the irrigation people also claim it. The matter is in the hands of the courts, where undoubtedly justice will be done." His voice suddenly hardened and the devils of laughter beat a hurried retreat to the back of his cold eyes.

140

"I tell you flatly it *is* silly," he said. "And by your attitude you are playing into the hands of unscrupulous individuals who would like nothing better than to see serious trouble of some sort come from it.

"I think," he concluded, "that it would be a fine thing for you to shake hands and forget your differences. Even the two strange dogs sometimes sniff noses and walk off together."

Again both engineer and cattleman had to grin.

"Oh, what's the use!" wailed Beckley. "There's just no sense in arguing with him; you can't win." He shoved his big hand across the table. Clark gripped it and they shook solemnly.

And at that moment an astounded Sheriff Medford walked in to stare unbelievingly at the tableau presented.

"Come on over, Tobe," Slade called. "We're having a little celebration."

"Yep," said Beckley as the sheriff approached. "We're discussin' dogs . . . tryin' to figure which one can sniff the hardest."

"I always calc'lated you to be loco, and now I know it," sighed the sheriff as he sat down. "All right, call off your dogs and let's have a drink."

As they discussed the drinks, Slade asked

a question,

"What judge is handling the land suit matter?"

"Judge Arbaugh," Beckley replied.

"Sure, he's holding court in town right now," Medford interpolated. "You know him, Walt, an old *amigo* of yours."

"Why?" Beckley asked.

"I was just wondering," Slade said, "if the matter couldn't be settled out of court. Suppose you, Mr. Beckley, would deed the land, which you don't really need, to the irrigation people, who do need it, in exchange for a block of stock in the project?"

"Why . . . why I can't say as I'd have any objections to such an agreement," replied Beckley.

"And you, Mr. Clark?" Slade asked.

"I am sure my company would welcome such a settlement," Clark answered.

"Okay," Slade said. "I'll see Arbaugh tomorrow. I'm sure he will approve."

"He will, when you tell him to," grunted the sheriff.

A little later, Slade said, "Pardon me a moment, will you please? I think Gorty wants to see me."

As he crossed the room to where the owner stood expectant, Beckley asked the sheriff, "Just what is he, anyhow?"

"Among other things," broke in Clark, "one of the finest engineers that ever showed in Texas."

"And one of the finest men," added Beckley.

"Right on both counts," said the sheriff. "Listen to him and you'll never go wrong."

Both his hearers nodded emphatic agreement.

It was Gorty's turn to ask a question when Slade reached him.

"Everything okay, Mr. Slade? I was a mite worried when I saw those two together; bad blood between them."

"Perhaps there was, but now all that's between them are a couple of glasses that need refilling," Slade smiled.

"And *I'll* take care of that!" Gorty declared. "Bert, my private bottle," he told the head bartender.

After they had done justice to the owner's offering, Beckley suggested to Clark,

"How'd you like to come over and meet my boys? I think it would be a good notion for them and your boys to get together, in the right way."

"I can't think of anything better," agreed Clark. "Let's go!"

At the table, Medford shook his head at Slade and repeated something he had often said . . .

"I don't know how you do it! I don't know how you do it!"

"Here's a quote for you that I believe applies," Slade answered. " 'Give the people light and they will find their own way.' "

"I suppose so," grumbled the sheriff. "But there ain't many who know how to use the lantern."

13

Slade glanced around the busy room. The bar was crowded, every gaming table occupied. The roulette wheels spun wildly. The dance floor was jam-packed.

"Looks like your prediction of a wild night wasn't far off," he observed. "Still quite early and Laredo is already beginning to howl."

"And she'll howl louder as the night goes on," Medford replied gloomily. "I like things jumpin', but I'm scairt they're liable to jump a mite too high before morning. There'll be trouble sooner or later, you watch. And I'm in the middle."

" 'A policeman's lot is not a happy one,' " Slade quoted smilingly. "But don't bother your head too much about it. After all, Laredo does have a police force that is supposed to help keep order."

"Those flat-foots couldn't keep order at an old maids' picnic!" snorted the sheriff with the oldtime cowman's scorn for town dwellers. "All they're good for is to hustle sidewalk-spitters. Holed up in some rum-hole right now, I betcha."

Slade did not think so but refrained from comment.

"So you have eliminated Beckley as a suspect, eh?" the sheriff remarked.

"To all practical purposes, I eliminated him the first time I spoke with him," Slade replied. "He just didn't fit into the picture. As I have often said, there is no such thing as a criminal physiognomy or a criminal type. But criminal acts almost universally follow a pattern, which must be seriously considered where the suspect is concerned. Beckley is a man of some education, fair intelligence, and has been around a bit. But he does not give any indications of possessing the subtle ingenuity that characterized the depredations committed here, such as firing of the steamer, the planting of the dynamite in the Albemarle safe, and trying to kill me with the water jet of a hydraulic giant. Those were the acts planned by a highly intelligent and deviously criminal mind. Beckley's methods would be direct. He and his hands might have gotten drunk, shot up the irrigation workers' camp or overturned a steam shovel, or something like that. Which would be the extent of his activities."

"Sorta agree with you there," admitted Medford. "Have you any notion who *is* responsible?"

"A very definite notion, but I'm not ready to talk about it just yet," Slade answered. "So far I have no proof."

"You'll get it," the sheriff declared confidently. "That is, if you manage to stay alive."

"I'm still alive, and that's what counts," Slade replied carelessly. The sheriff snorted and ordered another drink. Slade settled for another cup of coffee.

"Beckley's hands and the irrigation boys are whoopin' it up for fair," chuckled Medford. "And him and Clark are jabberin' away together like long lost brothers. Well, guess I'd better mosey out and look things over. Going to stay here a while?"

"Yes, for a while," Slade decided.

"Okay, I'll be seeing you," Medford said and ambled out. Slade sat back in his chair, smoking and studying the patrons.

Business was booming but the crowd, while noisy, appeared to be good natured and fairly well behaved. Gradually he concluded there was nothing to be learned in the Montezuma; like the sheriff, he'd go out and mosey around a bit and see what he could see.

Before leaving, he approached the engineer, who was engaged in animated conversation with Beckley.

"Mr. Clark," he said, "if convenient with you, I'd like to have you take a little ride with me day after tomorrow. There is something I have to show you that I believe you will find interesting."

"With pleasure," the engineer returned. "I'll meet you here day after tomorrow, say at two o'clock?"

"That will be okay," Slade replied. "Be seeing you, Beckley."

With a wave to Gorty who was busy as a packrat in a jewelry store, he left the Montezuma for the crowded and equally noisy street.

Everybody appeared peaceful and having a good time. Might be different later, after a little more redeye was consumed.

Gradually he worked his way to the river front. Here he walked warily, paying attention to his surroundings, for this section of the town had a questionable reputation. Several times he noted eyes glint toward him in a speculative manner. Evidently, however, their owners concluded it wasn't safe to monkey with him, for nobody approached him, nobody spoke.

As he progressed, the lighting grew poorer, the numerous saloons dingier. The ever-present racket developed a raucous tone. Occasionally voices rose high in dispute. The shrill laughter of women sounded through the rumbling uproar.

The river moaned and muttered against the piling, its star-dimpled waters throwing off sparkles of light. The long bulk of the International Bridge loomed darkly against the sky.

It was an eerie setting that always gave the impression of exuding a tense expectancy, like to a crouching monster waiting, waiting! The clean boisterousness of the upper town was lacking here, replaced by a sinister growl that rose and fell but was never absent. Here assembled the dregs of the community and its visitors.

Finally he entered a saloon that from the outside looked even dingier than average. However, when he stepped in a waiter met him with a bow and a pleasant smile.

"Bar or table, sir?" he asked courteously.

Slade glanced at the bar, which was crowded. "A table, I believe," he decided. "That small one over by the wall will do nicely."

The waiter bowed again and led the way to the table, from which Slade had a view of the bar and the swinging doors as well. The waiter took his order and hurried off. Slade let his eyes travel along the bar.

Suddenly his gaze fixed. Standing at the bar, near the far end, were two men. One was Amos Rolf, the purchasing agent. The other, wearing rangeland clothes and packing a gun, was the nozzleman who tried to kill him with the hydraulic giant.

The two men were engaged in conversation, apparently oblivious to their surroundings. Rather, Rolf was talking, the other listening, nodding his head from time to time as one receiving and understanding instructions.

Rolf spoke a few more words, received a nod in reply. He turned abruptly and left the saloon, glancing neither to right nor to left. Slade felt sure the agent hadn't seen him against the shadowy wall. He hesitated then decided to stay and keep an eye on the nozzleman, who kept glancing at the clock. He felt that if something was in the wind, the fellow would play an active part. He sipped his drink and waited.

It was a fairly long wait. He ordered another drink, paid the tab and tipped the waiter generously. Fully half an hour passed before the nozzleman made a move. He gave the clock a last glance and sauntered out.

Slade got up and followed.

On the street he had no difficulty spotting his quarry and followed, keeping well back. He was confident that with his own extraordinary eyesight he could keep the fellow in view and himself remain unnoticed.

A couple of blocks down the street and the fellow slowed. Another moment and two more men in cowhand garb stepped from a doorway and joined him. There was a moment of conversation and then the three hurried on, heading in the general direction of Grant Street.

Suddenly they turned into a dark alley which Slade instantly recognized as the one the far end of which opened just across from Miguel's cantina. He quickened his pace, reached the alley. Taking a chance, he slipped in. The narrow lane was black dark. Brushing against the building walls, hands close to his guns, he glided forward noiselessly.

Another moment and he sighted the quarry, outlined against the light from the street. They were watching the street expectantly, and Slade was sure that intent regard boded no good for somebody.

But what in blazes! Did the hellions figure he was in the cantina and were waiting for him to come out, with another attempt at drygulching him in mind? No! That just didn't make sense, but there was little doubt but that they were up to something. He eased ahead a few more steps, to where he had a view of the street for some distance, and waited. This time he didn't have long to wait.

Suddenly three men, headed down Grant Street in the direction of Miguel's cantina, loomed under a street light. Slade recognized Rolf, Ernest Clark, the engineer, and Dick Beckley, the Triangle C owner. They walked in leisurely fashion, talking together.

As they neared the cantina, Rolf abruptly took a couple of quick steps that put him in front of his companions. And *El Halcón* understood. He flicked both guns from their sheaths and his voice rang out:

"Elevate! You're covered!"

The three men in the alley mouth whirled toward the sound of his voice, guns in hand.

Slade took no chances. He fired right and left at the none-too-plainly-seen target. There was a gasping cry and one of the drygulchers fell. The other two fired a couple of shots that missed, whirled and darted out of the alley, one heading up the street, the other down. Slade bounded in pursuit, but he had to skirt the wounded man thrashing about on the ground and lost precious seconds. When he bulged from the alley mouth, the two fugitives were some distance away.

Across the street, Dick Beckley instantly sized up the situation. He whipped out his gun and fired at each of the drygulchers in turn. A yelp of pain echoed the reports, but both men kept going. Another instant and they whisked around corners and out of sight. Slade knew it was useless to try and overtake them in the maze of crooked streets and alleys. He crossed the street, after a glance back that assured him the man on the ground was incapable of doing any damage; he was hard hit.

Clark looked dazed. Beckley was swearing wholeheartedly and stuffing cartridges into the cylinder of his gun. Rolf's face was convulsed with anger. Suddenly he flickered a gun from a shoulder holster and fired two quick shots into the alley mouth.

"I saw something move in there," he told his startled companions.

"I don't think you'll see any more movement there," Slade said dryly as he turned back and recrossed the street. To himself he murmured: "Talk about hairtrigger reaction!"

14

Reaching the alley, he dragged a body into the light. He was not particularly surprised to recognize the nozzleman. *He* certainly wouldn't do any talking. One slug, Slade's, had smashed his shoulder low down. A second had drilled him dead center . . . straight through the heart!

Men were boiling out of the cantina. Foremost was Pancho, hand on the haft of his long knife.

"What is it, *Capitan,* are you safe?" he asked anxiously.

"I'm okay," Slade replied. "See if you can find the sheriff and bring him here."

"Of a certainty," replied Pancho. He and several of his companions hurried off in quest of Medford. Slade turned to find Amos Rolf beside him, peering at the nozzleman's dead face.

"Mr. Slade!" he exclaimed. "It is the fellow who came so near to injuring you by his careless handling of that hydraulic nozzle. I fired him yesterday. Looks like he intended to even up the score."

"Possibly," Slade conceded.

Beckley and Clark joined them. " 'Pears you got into action just in time, Mr. Slade," said the rancher. "If you hadn't, I reckon one or more of us would have gotten it. How did you happen to be so handy?"

"I was taking a short cut through the alley and spotted those devils with guns in their hands and watching you fellows headed this way. I figured they were up to no good and that something should be done about it," the Ranger replied, which was near enough to the truth.

"Thank Pete you didn't waste any time," said Beckley.

"But why should somebody wish to kill us?" asked the bewildered Clark.

"We have enemies," Rolf answered the question, leaving Clark to draw his own conclusions. Beckley blundered a remark Slade wished he had kept to himself, "Hellion looks to be a cowhand."

"Why, so he does," said Clark and glanced questioningly at Slade, who shook his head the merest trifle. Clark seemed to understand, for he nodded.

"Well, I suppose that's the cantina across

the street you suggested we visit, Mr. Rolf," he said. "Guess we might as well go in and wait for the sheriff."

"Guess we could do worse," agreed Rolf. "Let's go. And thank you, Mr. Slade, for the part you played in the affair. I won't forget it."

When they entered, they found plenty of room at the bar, for most of the patrons were grouped around the body, trying to figure just what happened. So they lined up there. Slade waved to Marie, who shook her head resignedly and went on dancing.

With Pancho accompanying him, the sheriff arrived shortly. He and Slade repaired to where the body lay. At a nod from Slade, Pancho sauntered along behind.

"Listen," Slade told the Mexican knife-man, "Mr. Clark — you know the one I mean — is staying at the hotel off Montezuma Street tonight. When he leaves here, you and some of your boys ride herd on him till he gets there."

"Of a certainty, *Capitan,*" Pancho replied, asking for no explanation. When *El Halcón* told one to do something, one did it without questions.

An officious policeman was shooing the crowd away when they reached the other side of the street. Sheriff Medford shooed

156

him away.

"Sidewinder looks sorta familiar," he remarked, peering at the dead face. "But darned if I can place him."

"I hope you, or somebody, will," Slade said. "I'd like to know something of his background. And I sure wish he'd lived long enough to talk a little."

"You shoot too darn straight," grunted the sheriff.

"And so do some other folks," Slade replied dryly.

Medford shot him a questioning glance, but *El Halcón* did not elaborate, at that moment.

"I'll have some of Miguel's boys pack the carcass to your office," he said. "Put it on display."

"And listen, Tobe," he added in low tones as they turned away. "Station a deputy at the site of the irrigation project . . . you have plenty excuse for doing so, the things that have been happening. A trustworthy and able man. Tell him not to let Clark out of his sight a moment. Otherwise Clark will very likely be a dead man. I'll tell you everything later, when we get a chance to talk."

"Getting a line on things, eh?" muttered the sheriff.

"Yes, definitely," Slade answered. "But still not an iota of proof."

At the bar, they found the others regaling the highly interested Miguel with an account of what happened. A few minutes later, Rolf announced, "It's late; I'm heading for bed. Work to do tomorrow. Thank you again, Mr. Slade, for everything."

"Don't mention it, it was a pleasure," the Ranger replied, and meant it.

The sheriff ordered another drink. After emptying his glass, Clark said,

"Gentlemen, I'm also going to call it a night. Somehow, all of a sudden, I feel completely worn out. Too much excitement, I guess." He glanced admiringly at Slade.

"Nothing seems to affect your nerves," he remarked. "You look as chipper as a squirrel in a hickory-nut tree."

"Excitement of one sort or another has been developing in such frequent doses of late that it's growing a bit stale and commonplace," *El Halcón* smiled reply. "One can get used to anything, you know."

"Perhaps in your case," Clark conceded dryly. "I fear I'm not one of the hardy souls who thrive on such things."

"Stick around and you'll get used to it, too," observed the sheriff. "Just stay in Walt's company and you'll never complain

158

of lack of excitement; it just follows him around."

Clark laughed. "I'd say you have the right of it, Sheriff," he agreed. "Goodnight, Mr. Slade, and I wish to add my thanks to Mr. Rolf's . . . for everything."

With a smile and a nod he also departed, Beckley accompanying him.

"See you folks tomorrow . . . this afternoon, rather; way past midnight," he said.

As they passed through the swinging doors, Pancho, the knife man, and several of his *muchachos* also sauntered out; Slade had no fears for Clark's safety.

Medford glanced around. "Things 'pear to be quieting down quite a bit," he commented. "I see a table over there with nobody close to it."

"A good notion," Slade agreed, with a glance at Marie, who was still dancing, but watching the clock.

"So you've definitely lined somebody up, eh?" said the sheriff as they sat down. "Mind telling me who?"

"No," Slade answered. "Time you should know. It's Amos Rolf."

"Amos Rolf!" Medford repeated. "Walt, are you sure?"

"Yes, I am sure," Slade replied. One by one he recounted the incidents that pointed the finger of suspicion at the purchasing agent.

"Always just before something happened, he was in evidence, and in a significant manner, like when he tried to have the nozzleman kill me with the hydraulic giant. He went into a rage when the fellow failed, then tried to account for it by concern over my safety. That is his weakness, the only one I've been able to discover; he does not have complete control of his emotions. The nozzleman, I feel sure, was one of his key men, who doubtless was thoroughly conversant with his plans and aims.

"And does he think fast! Tonight he was afraid the fellow, badly wounded, would talk to save his own hide, so he took no chances and eliminated him at once. The other two? Just guns-for-sale hired to do a chore is my opinion of them.

"Last night, of course, clinched the case against Rolf. Now I know for sure Rolf is my man, but, as I said before, I still don't have any proof against him that will stand up in court." He paused for a moment, then resumed, "The element of coincidence might be said to enter into the picture last night."

"How's that?" the sheriff asked.

"In that I happened to enter that particular saloon at the particular moment Rolf was giving the nozzleman his instructions, which were to be put into effect when he persuaded Clark and Beckley to visit Miguel's cantina.

"Not so much coincidence, however. I had planned to visit several places among the riverfront in the hope of picking up some information."

Again he paused. "I am inclined to say, rather, that there is a Destiny that shapes things. A Something that directed my steps to that particular place at that particular time. I have observed its workings before."

The sheriff, who believed it to be true, nodded soberly.

"But why is he so anxious to kill Clark?" he asked.

"Because now that Clark is listening to me, he is in his way," Slade explained. "He made up his mind to eliminate Clark, and he'll do it eventually if we don't watch our step. He has some sort of a hold on Clark. Just what it is I am not sure, but I'm getting an idea. I expect Jim Dunn back here any day, now, and perhaps he can give a hand when that angle is concerned. Rolf, I'm convinced, is the field man for the Neches Waterway interests and is here to delay or frustrate the irrigation project. Starting

161

those rumors that got the cattlemen and the Zapata ranchers on the prod was part of his campaign. So was the firing of the steamer loaded with needed supplies for the project. The robbery of the Albemarle safe, under cover of the fire, was another. Those too-shadow inlet channels were still another. I know very well it was Rolf who estimated the depth, and Clark, perhaps doubtfully, went along with him. Clark gave it away by the remark he made, for no apparent reason — 'Mr. Rolf seldom makes a mistake.' Understand?"

"Guess I do," nodded the sheriff. "He's a shrewd and ornery article, all right."

"Yes, he's all of that, Slade agreed soberly. "Something hard to explain. A genius who somehow, somewhere took the wrong fork in the trail, Heaven alone knows why. Shrewd, resourceful, with a dominant personality, and utterly ruthless. With not the slightest regard for the sanctity of human life. The most difficult type for the law enforcement officer to deal with. But perhaps he'll slip, sooner or later."

"He will," the sheriff said. "Or rather, you'll make him slip. Of that I'm plumb sure."

Having changed to a street dress, Marie joined them and the conversation ended.

15

The next day, promptly at two o'clock, Ernest Clark showed at the Montezuma. Slade saddled up and they rode down Bruni Street to the river, where Slade pointed out the Indian Crossing and explained the formation to the engineer.

"When you continue your project westward past the town, behind that ledge will always be impounded water ready for you to draw off," he said. "No matter how low the river is, there will be a fine head of water back of the ledge. All you'll need is deep channels lined with tile to lead to your laterals. It will save you a great deal of work and heavy expense."

"Mr. Slade," said Clark, "you are absolutely right. Not understanding that formation as it stands, I would never have thought of it. We'll do just as you say, and I'm sure Mr. Rolf will approve."

Slade turned slowly to let his gaze rest on

the engineer's face.

"Mr. Clark," he asked, "why do you have to obtain Mr. Rolf's approval? As I understand the situation, you are the engineer in charge, while Mr. Rolf is just the purchasing agent for your company."

Clark hesitated a moment before he spoke. "Mr. Slade," he replied, "what I am going to tell you is strictly confidential. I am not supposed to reveal it to anybody, but I feel that you should know. Mr. Rolf is the personal representative of the president of my company . . . he has letters to that effect, which I took the precaution to confirm. He has the last say in any matter relative to the project."

"I see," Slade said thoughtfully. "And now, Mr. Clark, I am going to request that you regard as strictly confidential what I revealed to you concerning the Indian Crossing. I have my reasons for asking."

"I could hardly do otherwise than agree," Clark admitted.

"Speak of it to nobody, including Mr. Rolf," Slade added. Clark nodded his understanding.

"I will do just as you say," he promised.

"Okay," Slade said. "Now we'll ride the river north and west for a bit and I'll point out certain features the knowledge of which

164

you may find of value when you start working up here."

Not until he was back to where Sheriff Medford's alert deputy could keep an eye on him did Slade part company with the engineer, confident he would come to no harm, and return to Laredo to wrestle with the problem which confronted him. The problem of how to balk Amos Rolf and bring him to justice, which promised to be something of a chore.

A couple of quiet days followed. Then General Manager Dunn's private car rolled across the railroad bridge from Mexico and came to rest in Laredo. Dunn at once dispatched Sam to round up Slade.

"Well, now what?" he asked when they were seated with coffee and what Sam considered a snack.

Slade regaled the G.M. with an account of the doings of Amos Rolf, including a meticulous description of Rolf and his mode of operating. Dunn listened in silence, nodding his big head from time to time.

"There is little doubt in my mind but that Rolf has been connected with the Waterway people," Slade concluded. "I'm confident you can find out for sure. I contemplated sending Captain McNelty a wire, but I've a notion you can do an even better job. You are acquainted with the personnel of both outfits and shouldn't have too much trouble putting a tracer on Rolf. Find out, if possible, where he came from and whom he was with in the past, and how he managed to worm his way into the irrigation project.

"What has me puzzled," he added, "is how the ornery devil managed to get the president of the project company under his thumb, as it were."

"I'd say that question isn't hard to answer," replied Dunn. "The president of that company is all right, I've known him for years, but he's getting pretty old and isn't as alert as he once was. Wouldn't be too difficult for a man of Rolf's personality, armed with the recommendations the Waterway outfit would manage to finagle for him, to ingratiate himself with him and win his confidence. Appears to be no doubt as to Rolf's ability."

"No, there's no doubt as to that," Slade said. "He's an engineer and a good one, and he's got a head on his shoulders. I'll agree with you, he'd be able to put it across, and by the time the irrigation people caught on, it would be too late."

"Exactly," agreed Dunn. "By that time their backers, already nervous, would pull out and they'd be forced to abandon the project. Don't forget, there's a fortune at stake here, and Rolf isn't playing for peanuts. Okay, I'll do my best to give you a lift . . . to sorta even up for the more than one you've given me. Say, this business is a good deal like our rows with the M.K. outfit, isn't it? Well, with your help I was able to give those scalawags their comeuppance and perhaps we can make history repeat, as it were." He chuckled and glanced at the clock, which was set to railroad time.

"Be pulling out in a few minutes and heading east," he said. "I'll get busy right away. Good hunting!"

Slade left the private car convinced that the angle dealing with the corroboration of his own deductions would be quickly taken care of; when Jaggers Dunn set out to do something, he did it, and without delay.

He considered Dunn's explanation of Rolf's influence with the president of the Irrigation Company quite plausible. A smart hellion, whom Slade exposed, had once gotten into the confidence of Jaggers Dunn himself, and Dunn wasn't easy to fool.

Altogether, things appeared to be working out pretty well. Now he could go back to the routine business of running down Amos Rolf.

But the elusive Mr. Rolf didn't prove easy

to run down. Indeed, he appeared to have embarked on a period of good behavior. For nothing untoward happened during the next several days. The irrigation work progressed smoothly, and Slade grew heartily weary of hanging around Laredo, even with the consoling company of Marie Telo.

He cudgeled his brains in an endeavor to anticipate Rolf's next move, and got exactly nowhere. He was convinced that the wily devil had something in mind that he would put into effect at any moment, but, blast it, what?

Meanwhile Slade received a laconic and, to the casual reader, cryptic telegram:

WAS WITH WATERWAY. IMAGINE STILL IS. DRAW OWN CONCLUSIONS. LETTER FOLLOWING.

Slade had already drawn his own conclusions and was pleased to have them substantiated. Otherwise he experienced an irritating sense of frustration, and an uneasy feeling that he was being outwitted in the deadly game he and Amos Rolf were playing.

Rolf had the advantage of being able to strike anywhere, at any time, and in whatever manner he saw fit to employ. And unless he, Slade, was able to anticipate the move, it would very likely have a telling effect. Even, perhaps, on himself personally, for there was no doubt but that Rolf earnestly desired to get rid of him once and for all and as quickly as possible.

There was one point he felt pretty sure would react in his favor. He was confident that Rolf did not consider himself suspect. He *had* done a fine job of covering up, and Slade was convinced that the inordinate vanity of the man caused him to look with contempt on any snooping, self-serving owlhoot of the type he had classified Slade to be. It was a weakness not uncommon to the criminal element. And a weakness that might well prove Amos Rolf's undoing . . . the mistake of underestimating his opponent. Did Rolf know *El Halcón* was a Texas Ranger, the story might be different. Rolf was too intelligent to discount the ability of a Ranger. But so long as he did not realize he had to deal with a member of that illustrious body of law enforcement officers, he might well grow careless. Slade believed that sooner or later he would. That had been his experience more than once when pitted against an individual of the Rolf type. Amos Rolf's vanity was the vanity, verging on stupidity, that often makes able men prostitute their natural gifts by directing them into the wrong channels. Vanity and greed! Motivating forces of the outlaw mind, and its weakness.

All of which was comforting, when viewed in the abstract, but which did not provide a solution to the immediate problem — where would Rolf strike next, and how? Slade swore wearily and entered the Montezuma in quest of some coffee: maybe that would help.

It did, indirectly.

Full dark had fallen and Slade was sipping his second cup of coffee when Pancho, the Mexican knifeman, slipped through the swinging doors in his silent, unobtrusive way, as a great snake would do. He glanced about, glided rather than walked to Slade's table.

"Take a load off your feet and have a snort," the Ranger invited, motioning a waiter.

Pancho did so, with a smile and a nod. Slade waited. He knew the young *vaquero* had something to say and would talk when he was ready.

He did so, in Spanish, his voice low, in a round-about way as was his habit when imparting information, first asking a question.

"Is it not strange, *Capitan,*" he said, "that one would climb to a roof top in the dark and remain there?"

"Depends on circumstances, I suppose," Slade replied obliquely.

"Well, one did," said Pancho. "A *ladrone* often seen in Nuevo Laredo. He entered Miguel's cantina and as he drank gazed about as if in quest of someone. Knowing he was evil, when he departed I also departed. He circled the block, entered the alley that opens onto Grant Street. I followed, silently in the dark, within knife casting distance." Pancho paused to sip his drink, then continued, "There is a place where one can mount to the roof of that low, flat-topped building directly across from the cantina. He mounted, and there he remained. I thought *Capitan* should know."

"You thought right," Slade answered, having instantly sized up the probable meaning of the situation. "Let's take a walk."

They entered the alley by way of the Lincoln Street mouth and glided silently as shadows to almost the far mouth. Pancho paused.

"Here, *Capitan,*" he breathed.

Slade felt of the building wall and found that transverse beams provided a good simulacrum of a ladder. He had no difficulty reaching the roof. Peering ahead he saw the man, leaning against the low false front that reached to a little above his waist, gazing intently across the street to the cantina almost directly opposite. He held a gun in his hand, the barrel resting on the top of the false front.

A novel and ingenious way to stage a drygulching. He was invisible from the street below and had a clear view of the door; his attitude was one of tense expectancy.

Slade eased ahead a few steps and called softly,

"Waiting for somebody, *amigo?*"

He heard the man gulp in his throat as he whirled around, the gun jutting forward. Slade drew and shot, but just as he squeezed trigger, the fellow leaped sideways and ran with amazing speed across the roof, almost invisible in the gloom, leaped across an opening to another roof and vanished in the darkness. Slade blasted two more shots in his general direction but with little hope of scoring a hit.

"*Capitan,* are you safe?" Pancho called from behind him.

"I'm okay," Slade replied, "but the hellion escaped. Quiet, now, people are coming out to investigate the shooting. I don't think they can spot us up here."

They didn't, and after gazing up and down the street and nosing into the alley, they retired to the cantina, talking and gesturing. Slade and Pancho slipped to the ground, hurried up the alley and circled the block to the cantina.

"A thousand pities the *ladrone* escaped," said Pancho. "He would have murdered *Capitan.*"

"He intended to murder somebody, all right," Slade conceded.

"*Capitan,* without a doubt," Pancho declared conclusively.

"You're probably right," Slade admitted. *"Gracias, amigo!"*

"Think naught of it, *Capitan,*" Pancho answered. "It is the honor to serve *El Halcón,* the good, the compassionate, the friend of the lowly. Let us enter and drink!"

Marie regarded Slade accusingly as she joined them at a table.

"I know you were mixed up in it somehow," she said.

"Yes, but thanks to Pancho, I came out of it all right," Slade replied.

"Tell me," she ordered.

He did. Marie turned to the *vaquero.* "Pancho, I could kiss you!" she said.

For the first time, Slade saw something

like fright cross Pancho's impassive features.

"Women I fear," he said, and drew back.

"Pancho, I fear you are a bit of a misogynist," Slade chuckled.

"No," said Pancho, "I am Mexican."

Marie tossed her curly head. "My kisses will not go begging," she retorted.

Pancho grinned, his teeth flashing white in his dark face. "The hours till the dawn are many," he murmured suggestively. Marie wrinkled her pert nose at him.

16

The promised letter from Jaggers Dunn arrived the following day. Slade read it with intense interest. There was no mention of Rolf's name, but the intimation was clear.

Was with the Wentworth people. After that, International Hydraulics. Impeccable reputation. Joined Brazos River Conservation and Reclamation. Quit after acrimonious political wrangle that denied him deserved promotion. Next appeared with the Neches Waterway outfit in an advisory capacity. Quit and dropped out of sight, to reappear at Laredo. Again, draw your own conclusions.

Slade drew them. He believed that the explanation of Rolf's deviation was contained in the "denied him deserved promotion." Not too strange that a man like Rolf, embittered, seething with a sense of injustice, and seeking revenge on society in general, should take the wrong fork of the trail. A pity, but such things happened, and there appeared to be no way of preventing it. *El Halcón* sighed, and burned the letter.

To be considered also, of course, was the great emolument that would accrue did Rolf accomplish what he set out to do. Amos Rolf was playing for high stakes.

Work on the project was booming. Everything going smoothly, no difficulties encountered. Too smoothly, Slade felt.

For the river decided to take a hand, and when the Rio Grande really goes on the rampage, it is something to contend with.

The river began to rise, slowly but steadily. As a result, Slade sent a telegram north in an endeavor to learn weather conditions around the head waters of Devil and Pecos Rivers. The answer was that it was raining hard with no indications of a letup anyways soon, which gave the Ranger considerable concern. He contacted Ernest Clark and told him, "Unless you act, you are in for trouble. All indications point to a regular sockdolager of flood waters roaring down from the west. If it develops to what it appears it's going to, without precautions taken to avert such a catastrophe, all the work you have done, along with your camp and your equipment, will be washed away. Here is what you should do . . . cut channels below the present site of the project to drain off the excess water onto the lowlands there, where it will do no harm."

It had become second nature to the engineer to defer to Slade. "All right," he replied. "I'll give the orders right away."

"And keep my name out of it," Slade cautioned. "*You* are making the decision."

"Very well," agreed Clark, and hurried off to make the needful preparations.

That night, however, he was back in Laredo wearing a worried expression.

"Mr. Rolf says it isn't necessary," he explained. "He says there is no danger and it would be just a waste of time and labor. In other words, he countermanded my orders."

"Very well," Slade said. "Sit tight and don't argue with him. I'll see what I can do."

The result of that interview was an urgent telegram to General Manager James G. Dunn in far off Chicago. It concluded: SEE WHAT YOU CAN DO.

The result of the telegram was that three days later the Winona, Jaggers Dunn's private car, rolled into Laredo over the M. P. Line.

"Blasted jerkwater railroad!" grumbled Jaggers. "We had one heck of a time making connections. Otherwise we would have been here sooner."

Accompanying Dunn was a benign, white-haired gentleman who was introduced as the president of the company handling the irrigation project.

After the amenities were over, including full appreciation of Sam's culinary efforts, Slade outlined the situation as it stood, for the president's benefit.

"And if those channels are not excavated without delay, sir, you are inviting disaster," he concluded.

Before the president could answer, Dunn put in . . .

"Bright, if Walt says to dig those channels, dig 'em. There's no better engineer in Texas and I've never known him to be wrong in such a matter. Dig 'em!"

The president nodded. "Mr. Slade," he said, "as I understand the situation, Mr. Clark, the engineer favors them, while Mr. Rolf maintains they are not needed."

"Mr. Rolf is perhaps not thoroughly familiar with the vagaries of the Rio Grande and consequently can make a mistake," was Slade's evasive answer. Dunn shot him a quick look. Slade nodded slightly. Dunn's mouth set in grim lines.

"Walt has already saved you a lot of time and money by rectifying one of your Mr. Rolf's mistakes," he said. "Let me tell you about it."

Followed an account of Slade's activities.

The president had a winning smile. Now he turned it on Slade.

"Mr. Slade," he said, "I think my company could use you."

"No you don't," Jaggers instantly vetoed the suggestion. "I've got him hogtied so far as signing on with anybody but me. When he is ready, he signs up with *me.*"

The president chuckled. "I learned years ago not to argue with Jim," he said, "Doesn't get you anything."

"And I learned quite a while back not to argue with *him,*" grunted Dunn, nodding to Slade. "You can't win."

The president chuckled again. "Okay, Jim," he said, "hire us a couple of horses and we'll ride down and look things over. As Mr. Slade says, delay might be disastrous."

"I have one request to make, sir," Slade said. "Please do not make mention of my name in connection with the affair. After looking over the situation, and being familiar with the river, *you* will make the decision. I have my reasons for asking."

"And I imagine they are good reasons," conceded the president. "Very well, Mr. Slade. If you do not desire to take the credit undoubtedly due you, I will do as you say. What I wish is that you would take charge of the project, complete charge."

"Thank you, sir," Slade replied.

But even as he spoke, the president saw his steady eyes look off into the far distances. He sighed, a trifle wistfully. Perhaps he was thinking of his own hair and wrinkled hands.

For in his youth, he too had been a wanderer.

Before nightfall, steam shovels were gouging, compressors chattering and picks thudding, to continue without a letup through the dark hours. And before another night of rain and blackness closed down, the growl and mutter of the swiftly rising river confirmed Slade's judgment.

But the flood water that was hammering the International Bridge with debris and inundating parts of Nuevo Laredo was thundering through the completed channels to spread out on the lowlands below the site of the project operations. The project was safe.

"Well, we stymied another of Rolf's schemes," Slade told Shadow when he visited the big black. "But we haven't stymied him personally, not by any manner of means. And that resourceful and inventive mind of his will figure some other way to make trouble, on that you can rely. Just you wait and see!"

Shadow munched oats and did not comment. So Slade left the stable and made his way through the driving rain to Miguel's cantina.

Now the Rio Grande was really showing what it could do. The International Bridge quivered from end to end under the impact and people began to wonder anxiously if the bridge might go out.

"I told them how to remedy the condition the last time I was here," Slade remarked to Marie. "Do away with those solid steel side sheets and replace them with removable aluminum railings. Aluminum is strong but very light. With the railings, it would require less than half an hour to pack the side sections to safety. Stripped that way, the bridge would present virtually no obstruction to the current and its floating debris, which now impounds the waters and floods Nuevo Laredo. Perhaps after this scare they'll do it."

Incidentally, they did, some time later.

"Before this is over the bridge will be submerged until only the tops of the high lamp-posts will be visible," he added.

Which was just what happened. And the lower sections of Nuevo Laredo suffered disastrous flooding.

Despite the elements, Miguel's cantina was doing an extremely good business. The bar was crowded and so was the dance floor. Most of the tables were occupied. The roulette wheels were spinning merrily. Players were wrangling amicably at the faro bank.

"With nothing to do outside, everybody comes in where it's snug and dry," Marie hazarded.

"Looks that way," Slade agreed.

Marie returned to the dance floor. Slade leaned back in his chair with coffee and a cigarette. For a while he watched the games and the dancers and listened to the beat of the rain on the window panes. Gradually, however, he grew restless, weary of the noise and inaction. Finally he donned his slicker, buttoned it tight at the throat, and met Marie at the edge of the dance floor.

"I'm going out for a little stroll," he told her. "I want to have a look at the river."

"Be careful," she urged, "it's a wild night.

One blessing, though, unlikely anybody will be prowling around waiting for a chance to trade shots with you."

"Highly unlikely," he agreed. "Be seeing you soon."

"I'll be waiting for you," she said.

Outside, the wind-driven rain almost blinded him for a moment. It was not cold, however, and he didn't mind the wet. Overhead the lightning flashed, the thunder rolled. Nearby the river also roared, luridly lit up from time to time by the lightning bolts.

The look of the river was far from satisfactory. It was a raging torrent and Slade estimated it was rising by at least a foot an hour, and it was unlikely that the crest would be reached until some time the following morning.

He pondered the possibility of it breaking through its banks west of the project. If it did, the rushing water would quickly widen and deepen the breach. The effect on the project would be devastating.

Little chance of that, though; the banks were high and solid and heavily grass-grown.

But suppose one of the still dry inlet channels had been excavated to a point too close to the bank and had weakened it? His remembrance of them told him that was not the case. No danger there. Indeed, he could conceive of nothing that could possibly go wrong.

Nevertheless he was experiencing a growing disquietude. An uneasy feeling that something was not as it should be. A presentiment, very unpleasant, of impending evil. He tried to shake it off, dismiss it from his mind as nothing but an over-active imagination, and failed signally. It persisted, strengthened, clamoring for recognition, driving its barbs of warning deeper and deeper into his brain.

Finally he gave up. "I won't have any peace till I take a look down there," he growled aloud. "Oh, well, as Barnum said, there's one born every minute! And when they were picking the fool tree I guess they looked on me as a prime specimen."

He traversed the rain drenched streets and got the rig on the big black.

"I'm playing a plump loco hunch, horse," he said. "And if you sprout fins, you'll know who to blame." With which he rode out into the rain.

17

But rain or no rain, Shadow was glad of a chance to stretch his legs, being heartily weary of being cooped up inactive. He snorted gaily as he breasted the watery gale, his hoofs thudding and sloshing on the eastward trail that ran close to the river bank.

Overhead was utter blackness, save when the jagged streaks of lightning blazed the sky and bathed all things in a lurid, bluish glow. One minute the darkness was as solid as if it were the black marble blocks of a tomb. The next, it was swept away by hands of flame that sparkled the tossing waters of the Rio Grande and alchemized the rain drops to fiery gems.

Yes, it was a wild night, with every promise of growing wilder. And the very fact that he rather enjoyed it convinced Slade that he was indeed one of those mentioned by the great showman . . . utterly terrapin-brained, crazy as a coot full of hooch. He chuckled and rode on. The rain was descending as hard as ever, but the lightning flashes were less frequent.

He was a mile or so west of the project site and its big camp when he stiffened in the saddle, peering through the rain.

Atop the high river bank, perhaps two hundred yards distant, was a light. A light not of the intermittent lightning bolts, for it glowed steadily except when it winked now and then, as if something had momentarily obscured it.

"What in blazes!" Slade wondered. "Who'd have any business up there at this time of night, and such a night! Shadow, this will bear a mite of investigating. Take it easy, now."

Abruptly that mysterious sixth sense that develops in men who ride much alone and warns of peril where none, apparently, exists, was setting up its clamor in his brain. A warning he had learned not to disregard. He unbuttoned his slicker and, heedless of the rain, swept it back until it was free of his gun handles. Slowing Shadow's gait, he rode forward. Soon his extraordinarily keen eyes could make out the shadowy forms of three men moving about the light, which was cast by a big lantern. In the gloom he could not ascertain what they were doing.

He eased Shadow ahead until he was perhaps thirty paces distant from the light and the shadowy figures when the contrary lightning took a notion to blaze, making the scene as bright as day.

Slade heard a startled exclamation of warning, rising clear above the rumble of the river, instantly drowned by the thunder boom. He hurled himself sideways from the saddle as a gun spurted fire and a slug whizzed past. The dark rushed down like a thrown blanket.

Flattened on the soaked grass, Slade drew and shot with both hands. A yelp of pain and a torrent of curses echoed the reports. The three shadows vanished from the narrow circle of lantern light. Slade lay motionless a moment, peering and listening. He heard a thud of swift hoofs fading into the distance. And at the same instant he saw something. Something that sent him scrambling to his feet and racing toward the river . . . a flickering flower of fire crawling along the crest of the bank!

A lighted fuse, with undoubtedly a stick or sticks of capped dynamite at the end of it!

Panting to the top of the bank, Slade saw by the lantern light that his guess was correct. He reached for his knife, then remembered he had loaned it to Marie. And he dared not try and jerk the fuse from the cap.

Flinging himself on the ground, he seized the fuse, as near the cap as he could, and chewed frantically.

The tough fiber stubbornly resisted even his strong teeth. And the flower of fire crept closer and closer.

Madly he ripped and tore at the fuse. Another moment and the fire would reach the cap. The sparks spurted into his face. He endured the pain and made a last frenzied effort, putting all his strength in his champing jaws.

The fuse parted, with the core of fire bursting through the free end. Slade cast the smoking thing aside and for a minute or two lay prone on the ground, his face beaded with sweat that was colder than the rain.

Recovering somewhat, he moved the lantern closer, and whistled under his breath. There were fully a score of dynamite sticks expertly placed. They would have blown a gap in the bank yards wide and yards deep. The rushing torrent would have quickly completed the job and a mighty flood would have roared down the slope to drown the site of the project. Then men sleeping in the camp would have been lucky to escape with their lives. Very probably many would not have escaped.

The callous, inhuman devil! Taking a chance on mass murder to glut his itch for vengeance and his lust for gain! Slade drew a deep breath and went to work to carefully remove the dynamite. After making sure he had overlooked none, he hurled the cartridges, one by one, into the river. He didn't care to pack the stuff to town with him.

Really there was nothing to be gained by doing so. *He* knew that three men had tried to blow the bank and let the river through, but he didn't know who they were. There was no doubt in his mind as to who had instigated the attempt, but he had no proof. To the devil with it!

He did pack the lantern along against the chance that it had been purchased in Laredo and the more unlikely chance that Sheriff Medford could learn who sold it and to whom.

"Well, Shadow," he said as he swung into the saddle, "the hunch paid off despite your sneering. So tighten the latigo on your jaw a bit and don't go making big medicine. Believe the rain is letting up, and the wind is undoubtedly dying down. Let's go, horse. You need a rubdown and a helpin' of oats,

189

and I can do with some hot coffee. Afraid I'm going to have a blister or two on my face, but if that powder had let go there wouldn't have been enough of me to make a blister. Altogether, not such a bad night, after all."

With no further misadventure, he reached the stable and after caring for Shadow headed for Miguel's cantina.

As he knew very well she would, Marie instantly noticed the slight burns on his face, demanded an explanation and then treated them with a soothing ointment.

"Really I'm going to stop worrying about you," she declared. "You seem able to survive anything. Nice kitty! Nine lives to start with! How many you got left?"

After hot coffee and a bite to eat, Slade felt his normal self again. And he was not at all displeased with the night's work. Chalk up another setback for Rolf.

"Hope the sidewinder don't end up like the sheep, though," Slade told himself.

It was an axiom of the Old West that sheep could lose every battle but still win the war. Which the cattlemen who sought to bar them from the rangeland learned to their cost.

The river reached its crest the following morning, with no very serious damage reported. The International Bridge withstood the battering to which it was subjected, as did the less vulnerable railroad bridge. To the accompaniment of profanity in two languages, with some pungent Yaqui expletives thrown in for good measure, Nuevo Laredo drained off the water and dug out of the mud. Business resumed as usual.

Jaggers Dunn had elected to stay in Laredo and Slade had a few last words with him and the president of the irrigation company.

"It has been a great pleasure to know you, Mr. Slade," said the president. "I hope our acquaintanceship will endure indefinitely, and if you and Jim ever have a falling out, which I deem unlikely, you know where to come."

When he had Dunn alone for a few minutes, Slade related his experience of the night before.

"Yes, Rolf is my man, all right," he concluded. "But so far I haven't a smidgen of proof against him."

"You'll get it," Dunn predicted confidently. He hesitated, then . . .

"If you told the old man what you told me, he'd believe you and fire the horned toad."

"Yes, but that would just mean inflicting him on somebody else," Slade pointed out. "Also, he would then escape the punishment due him for the depredations he has committed here. And after all, I am a Texas Ranger, and the welfare of the people of Texas is my first and foremost consideration."

"Guess that's so," admitted Dunn. "Well, good hunting! I'll be seeing you. Oh, by the way, he tells me that they plan to greatly expand operations without delay, now that they've got the ground work laid, as it were. Should give your *amigo* more and better opportunities for hell raising."

"That's comforting," Slade smiled. "Well, it may also afford *me* greater opportunity. We'll see."

The private car with its booming locomotive in front, the bouncing caboose behind, rolled out of the yards and headed for Chicago, Dunn and the president waving their farewells from the rear platform. Slade went for a talk with Sheriff Medford.

He found the peace officer in his office and related, briefly, his adventure of the night before. Medford growled, swore, and shook his grizzled head.

"I sure wish somebody else had been along to give the real story of what happened," he complained. "I gather, from the way you tell it, that you just scared the hellions away with a couple of shots, picked up the dynamite and flung it in the river. A likely yarn! I suppose you got those spots on your face from raindrops, eh?"

Slade smiled and let it go at that.

"So the old president is keeping the horned toad on," observed Medford.

"Yes, he is a fair man and concedes that anyone may make a mistake, especially in a section where one is not thoroughly familiar with conditions. I did not consider it wise to acquaint him with Rolf's true character, at the moment."

"So the hellion is sitting pretty, until you tie something onto him, and may end up coming off scot-free," said Medford, gloomily.

"Perhaps," Slade admitted.

The storm had ended, the river was subsiding as swiftly as it rose and the sun was shining brightly in a sky of clear blue. Slade left the office and wandered about the streets for a while, thinking deeply.

As Medford said, Amos Rolf was at the moment sitting pretty. He, Slade, had been able to thwart some of his schemes and he believed that Rolf must be experiencing a certain irritating sense of frustration, which might possibly cause him to fly off the handle and commit some foolish act. That, however, was a contingency he mustn't bank on too heavily. Rolf was shrewd and farsighted, not given to making mistakes, and with a genius for doing the unexpected. So far he had been able to outthink the devil, to an extent, at least.

The night before was an example. His hunch, as he called it, was really the result of logical deductions, of carefully weighing possibilities that might provide opportunity. He had ridden toward the project site against the chance that Rolf might somehow turn the storm and the flooded river to his advantage. Which was exactly what Rolf tried to do, and only the timely arrival of the Ranger at the scene of operations had prevented the attempt from being successful. Slade had felt that if Rolf did plan to pull something, it would be somewhere in the vicinity of the project. He had reacted accordingly.

As Captain McNelty had often said, Walt Slade not only out-fought the owlhoots, he out-thought them. Which was the real secret of his outstanding success as a Texas Ranger.

Well, it was up to him to do some hard thinking right now, for it was a foregone conclusion that Amos Rolf's mental processes were not atrophied, far from it. No doubt but that *he* was also doing some hard thinking, and the results of his cogitations might be highly unpleasant for *El Halcón.*

Slade chuckled. Then, as an afterthought, he repaired to the stable, where he had left the lantern used by the dynamiters, secured it and returned to the sheriff's office.

Medford looked the thing over and nodded. "Only two or three stores in town that have 'em for sale," he said. "I'll look 'em up and see if I can learn anything. Might prove a clue."

"I doubt it," Slade replied. "But we mustn't pass up any bets." He tackled the streets and the sunshine again.

18

A few years before, a visitor had described Laredo as a very plain city whose prevailing style of architecture utilized stone or sun-dried brick walls and thatched roofs, a very plain city, drab in appearance.

Now, however, that was rapidly changing; there was new construction everywhere. According to a preconceived plan, its growing business section was of white face brick and stone buildings that dazzlingly reflected the sunshine and gave emphasis to an atmosphere of cleanliness.

It was still, and probably always would be a town of contrasts. Streets of the business section gave way abruptly to wide avenues where fine residences were already going up. While in some directions, older side streets featured adobe huts and squat houses of limestone. These structures were, for the most part, in good repair despite their age. The door and window casings were painted in splashes of brilliant color. There were most always flowers in a tiny square of garden — roses, geraniums, bluebonnets and daisies. Also, ligustrums, oleanders, and bougainvillia shrubs.

Already the custom house was reporting great volumes of merchandise from across the Border, including grain, cottonseed, vegetables and other raw products. And a distinctive item was developing. Quail trapped in Mexico were being shipped throughout the United States for restocking game preserves. In return, machinery of various sorts and shoes and clothing were exported to the land south of the Rio Grande.

Yes, Laredo was an up and coming pueblo, and with the impetus given its development by the irrigation project would bring it rapidly to the fore amid Border towns. Slade believed that before so very long, more than fifty percent of all freight crossing the International Border would be handled through the Laredo port. He was right.

Just the same, Laredo was still a frontier town, still primarily a cattle country town, and plenty wooly. Slade chuckled at the thought, leaned against a convenient lamp post and rolled a cigarette with the slim fingers of his left hand, meanwhile pondering his next move.

Abruptly he recalled promising Dick Beckley, the Triangle C owner, to pay him a visit when he got a chance. Well, this looked like a good chance. About six miles to the east was his ranchhouse, Beckley had said. He glanced at the sun. The afternoon was still not very far along. He could make it easily quite a while before sunset. And a ride back under the stars wouldn't go bad. Like Shadow, he was getting a bit tired of being "cooped up". The trails and the wastelands were beginning to whisper over his shoulder.

Getting the rig on Shadow, he rode east, remembering that Beckley had mentioned that his casa was an old gray building plainly visible from the trail. Shouldn't have any trouble spotting it.

He turned off at the site of the irrigation operations for a few minutes and saw Clark and Rolf inspecting a steam shovel that apparently was not working just right. Rolf waved his hand but did not approach, turning his attention back to the shovel.

Clark did come over for a word. "Off on a jaunt?" he asked.

"Yes, over to Dick Beckley's holding, six miles to the east," Slade replied. "I promised to drop in on him when I got the chance, and I sort of feel the need of a ride. Be back in town tonight."

Clark chuckled. "Guess, after all, you're a born cattleman and not happy unless you're on horseback," he observed.

"Something like that, I reckon," Slade answered with a smile. "Be seeing you." He turned Shadow toward the trail. Clark went back to Rolf and the shovel.

It was a beautiful afternoon, just right for a ride, and Shadow, welcoming the chance to stretch his legs, stepped out briskly. They were passing over excellent rangeland and after a while Slade saw clumps of grazing cattle bearing the Triangle C brand, well fleshed beasts in good condition, improved stock.

Before long he also saw the barbed wire that fenced certain pastures, and on hillsides the white blotches that were Beckley's sheep. Both of which were regarded askance by the oldtimers of the section.

"But they'll have to yield, sooner or later," he told Shadow. "As I said before, there's no stopping the wheels of progress, even if elderly gents 'sot in their ways' think they can slow the hands of the clock. Can't be done, and altering the angle of the sun dial doesn't change the time of day."

A little later the trail ran through a long

and wide stand of thick and tall chaparral, where already, though the sun was still fairly high in the sky, the shadows were curdling. It continued for perhaps a mile and ended as abruptly as it had begun, something not uncommon in the section.

Slade had no difficulty locating the Triangle C ranchhouse, for as Beckley said, it was plainly visible from the trail. It was an old structure but in good repair. The same applied to the bunkhouse, corrals, barn and other out-buildings; Dick Beckley was a cowman, all right, and knew his business.

As Slade rode into the ranchhouse yard, Beckley himself came out the front door and shouted a greeting. He whooped for a wrangler who quickly appeared, was properly introduced to Shadow and led the big black to a stall in the barn and a helping of oats. Slade and the rancher entered the house together.

"So you made it!" said Beckley. "Sure glad you did. Sit down, I'll be with you soon as I tell the cook to fix us coffee and a snack to hold us till dinner time."

In the course of the conversation that followed, Beckley remarked, "Clark told me the irrigation company president okayed the land deal and that I'd receive my stock in a few days. I've a notion I made a good trade, thanks to you."

"No doubt but that you did," Slade assured him. "Eventually this section will be a garden spot and will pay big dividends to the investors. That wedge-shaped strip of land, which you didn't really need, would hamper operations. I felt sure they'd be glad to go along with your proposition, especially after Judge Arbaugh recommended it."

"Thanks to you again," chuckled Beckley. "The sheriff was right when he said the judge would do whatever you told him to do."

Several hours after dark, Chuck Perkins, the cowboy who got a steer's horn through his arm, arrived from town and greeted Slade warmly.

"A couple of fellers passed me on the trail, headed this way," Chuck observed. "Seemed to come from the irrigation project. Strangers to me. Sorta mean lookin' jiggers, I thought. Rode right by without speaking or looking at me, though I waved to 'em."

"Didn't hear anybody pass this way tonight," Beckley replied. "Might have missed them, though."

Slade said nothing, but looked thoughtful.

Shortly before midnight, Slade announced his intentions to head back to Laredo.

"A sorta lonely ride," objected Beckley.

"Don't you think you'd better spend the night with us . . . plenty of room."

"I desire to be in town early tomorrow," Slade answered. "Thanks for the invitation, but I figure I'd better get going."

"And there goes just about the finest man what ever spit on the soil," declared Beckley.

In the course of his ride to the Triangle C ranchhouse, Slade had given only superficial attention to his surroundings, for on the open prairie, mounted on Shadow, he knew nobody could approach near enough to do any damage.

Now, however, it was different and he rode watchful and alert. He couldn't get the two strangers who had passed Chuck Perkins and apparently had not passed the ranchhouse out of his mind. He was sure they had not ridden past the casa; his ears would have undoubtedly caught the sound of their horses' irons on the hard trail.

So he rode watchful and alert, carefully listening to and analyzing the call of night birds, and the movements of little animals. More than once, his observance of such things had saved him from disaster.

An almost full moon was peeping over the eastern hills, bathing the prairie in ghostly silver radiance, in which objects stood out hard and clear to Slade's eyes for a long distance.

Eventually he approached the belt of thicket. But before reaching it, the trail dipped into a depression that was almost a dry wash, for the steep slopes encroached on the trail and were higher than the head of a mounted man. Beyond the depression, the trail ran straight for more than a score of yards before entering the brush, shimmering in the still white flood of the moonlight. The depression was dark, for the moon had not risen high enough for its beams to penetrate the depths. The stretch of trail between the depression and the chaparral was bright as day.

He was some distance from the far end of the depression when he heard an owl whistling cheerfully. A coyote yipped answer. Doubtless both creatures were holed up in the beginning of the thicket, the coyote beneath the owl's tree. He knew that on such a moonlight night the bird and the little prairie wolf would continue to exchange opinions of each other indefinitely.

With a chuckle, Slade continued on his way. He was quite near the end of the depression when suddenly the owl's whistle changed to an irritated whine. The coyote ceased barking and at the same instant,

Shadow blew softly through his nose.

Slade quickly halted him and sat listening. "Now what shut up those critters so abruptly?" he wondered to the horse. "And you seem trying to tell me something," he added as Shadow again blew softly, his ears pricked forward.

Now the prairie was deathly still. Listening intently, Slade heard nothing, saw nothing save the glow of moonlight against the crest of the rise.

"But, horse, I don't like it," he whispered. "Something stopped that pair yelling at each other, something they don't understand and are afraid of, and with you acting up, I *sure* don't like it. A man riding that stretch of moon-bright trail would be a settin' quail for anybody holed up in the brush. Horse, I'm going to play a hunch again. Maybe a loco one. I hope it is. But I've got a notion it isn't. Anyhow, we're not going to take any chances."

Dropping the split reins to the ground, he dismounted. "Stay put, and keep quiet," he breathed. Cautiously and with some difficulty, he climbed the steep bank to the right, peered over it and saw nothing. The grass was tall and thick and would almost hide his body. He eased forward, flattened out and listened. Reassured by the continued silence, he crawled slowly ahead, keeping down as much as possible. Were there some hellions holed up in the brush, he felt pretty sure their attention would be focused on the trail.

After covering about a dozen yards on his stomach, he again paused, then turned and crawled toward the bristle of growth.

It was a ticklish business. If the drygulchers were really there and glanced in his direction, they might spot the movement of his body. Well, he'd have to take that chance. He crawled on, drawing nearer and nearer the edge of the thicket. The moonlight seemed to be getting brighter and his imagination could visualize the gun barrel swinging in his direction, murderous eyes glinting along the sights. The blaze of flame he would see, the report he quite likely wouldn't hear, a slug travelling faster than sound. He was sweating a little when he reached the grateful shadow of the brush with nothing happening.

Easing erect, he stood listening. And suddenly he heard a sound, a sound that removed all doubt from his mind — the muffled stamp of a horse's foot. Yes, the hellions were there. Now if he could only spot them before they spotted him! He slipped slowly and with the utmost caution through the thinning growth in the direction of the trail.

Abruptly, two shapes loomed almost beside him. His hands streaked to his gun. Then he relaxed; just a couple of horses tethered to branches. He eased ahead another stride and saw the drygulchers, two of them. They were standing at the edge of the growth, facing the trail. Which was all to the good, for here the overhead growth was quite thin and he, too, was outlined by splotches of moonlight.

Slade experienced a surge of hot anger. The devils meant snake-blooded murder, no less; he had a right to blow them from under their hats where they stood.

But he couldn't; he was a law enforcement officer, a Texas Ranger. He must give them the undeserved chance to surrender. He started to speak.

And at that moment one of the horses gave vent to an explosive snort.

The two men turned quickly toward the sound, guns in hand. Slade drew and shot. Weaving, ducking, swerving, he fought it out with the pair. A battle of moon-speckled shadows blasting death at one another through the gloom.

A slug ripped the leg of Slade's overalls, just touching the skin. A second turned his hat sideways on his head. One of the men crumpled up without a sound. His companion pitched forward on his face. Slade started forward, then went sideways in a cat-like leap. A bullet fanned his face as a gun belched fire from the ground. He hammered the prone form with bullets. There was a gasping cry, a gurgling groan, and the Ranger realized there was no more lead coming in his direction.

"Confound you! I think you'll stay dead this time!" he apostrophised the drygulcher who had very nearly caught him off balance by his quick-thinking trick of throwing himself on the ground.

Every nerve at hairtrigger alertness, he eased forward again, ready for instant action.

There was no need for it; both men were dead, the first drilled dead center, the second shot to pieces. Slade ejected the spent shells from his guns and replaced them with fresh cartridges. Then he dragged the two bodies into the light.

He couldn't be sure, but he believed they were the pair who had joined the nozzleman in the attempt to kill Ernest Clark and Dick Beckley from the alley mouth across from Miguel's cantina.

"Now I see it all . . . marvel of perspicacity," he told himself. "Rolf learned from Clark that I was heading for the Triangle C and would head back to Laredo tonight. Saw opportunity and took advantage of it. And if it hadn't been for an owl, a coyote, and a darned smart horse, it would very likely have worked. Well, it didn't, and that's all that counts. Hellion must be sorta running out of hired hands to take care of his chores of murdering for him — maybe!"

There was one bright spot in the sordid business: So far, Rolf had not succeeded in killing anybody, except the hydraulic giant nozzleman, who wasn't much of a loss. It was natural to Slade that he did not reflect it was only his own courage, farsightedness and ingenuity that had prevented Rolf from being in a position to carve quite a few notches in his gun stock, including one for *El Halcón* personally.

Emptying the dead men's pockets revealed nothing of significance save a rather large amount of money, which he replaced. Quite likely advance payment for murder. He leaned against a convenient trunk, rolled a cigarette. Now that everything was over, the reaction had set in and he was feeling quite a bit weary and let down. He smoked the brain tablet to a short butt, which he carefully pinched out and cast aside. Then he got the rigs off the two horses and turned them loose to fend for themselves. After which he returned to Shadow, who appeared quite unimpressed by the whole affair, mounted and rode on to town, confident there would be no more excitement during the remainder of the ride.

There wasn't. Reaching Laredo, he stabled Shadow and proceeded to Miguel's cantina.

When he entered, he found sitting in a chair with a snort on the table before him, a lanky, mustached gent.

"Figured you'd get back before closing time, which ain't far off," the sheriff said. "Well, out with it. I know darn well you've been into something. Another bullet hole in your hat."

Slade told him everything. The sheriff was too wearily disgusted to even swear.

"Anyhow, you're thinning out his bunch," he remarked. "I'd say you've just about cleaned 'em."

"Which, in a way, gives me something additional to worry about," Slade said.

"How come? Looks all to the good to me," puzzled Medford.

"I mean that there is probably a limit to how much money the waterway people will advance Rolf," Slade explained. "And he'll have to have money to hire more guns. I'm convinced he's in this thing, fight to the finish with no holds barred, and that if necessary, he'll go it on his own. What we may have to look out for now is a nice little bank robbery or something of that sort, with murder quite likely as a sideline."

This time Medford managed to get out a cuss word or two. "I expect you're right — you always seem to be," he admitted. "Well, here comes your gal; reckon she's finished for the night. And so am I. Just listening to you wears me out complete. Yes, I'll ride over and pick up the carcasses, if that coyote and the owl haven't beat me to it."

19

Sheriff Medford brought in the bodies the following afternoon and placed them on exhibition. This time with better results than average. Several bartenders and a saloon-keeper or two from both Laredo and Nuevo Laredo recalled the pair as unsavory characters who hung about the riverfront rum-holes, apparently without steady employment but always having money to spend.

"Begins to look like Rolf is hiring some local *ladrones*," Slade observed to the sheriff. "Guns-for-hire type always to be found along the Border. May work to our advantage. That sort is seldom long on intelligence and likely to make a slip. Last night's attempt at a drygulching was a sample. They would have done much better to wait well back along the trail in the brush, where there would have been less chance of them being spotted."

Doc Beard held an impromptu and short

inquest that quickly exonerated Slade of all blame. Laredo's Chief of Police, plump, jolly, but with shrewd little eyes set deep in rolls of fat, shook hands and congratulated him. He twinkled the eyes.

"Sorta got a notion, Mr. Slade, that you might have had something to do with the *accidents* suffered by certain gents of similar caliber hereabouts of late. If you ever feel the need of a job, come around and see me. Be glad to put you on.

"Oh, by the way, wasn't it you, about a year back, who recommended that the bridge's solid steel side sheets be replaced by aluminum railings that can be quickly removed and packed off? Thought so. Well, thought you might like to know that the boys are getting busy at it pronto. The flood the other night scared the hell out of 'em."

Said Sheriff Medford, after the chief had departed, "He's not a bad sort; does a pretty good job, considering what he has to work with.

"I forgot to tell you," he added, "but Rolf dropped in for a look at the bodies. I asked him if he'd ever seen them before and he said he hadn't. Wonder why the devil he did that?"

"I would say to ascertain the nature of their wounds," Slade replied.

"Why?"

"To see if there was any chance that they might have done some talking before they died," Slade explained. "Well, he's resting easy on that score, after one look."

"The horned toad thinks of everything!" growled the sheriff.

"He sure doesn't miss many bets," Slade agreed.

"He'll miss one sooner or later," snorted Medford. "One that has to do with the hot end of a bullet or the noosed end of a rope, the ornery cross between a rattlesnake and a hyderphobia skunk!"

Slade hoped the sheriff was right. So far, however, the elusive Mr. Rolf had managed to avoid both, and Slade still didn't have the slightest idea how to drop his loop on that slippery customer.

Telling Medford he would be back before long, he went out to walk the streets again. After strolling about a bit, he sauntered down Bruni Street to the river and stood contemplating the Indian Crossing. The river had fallen very rapidly and patches of the ledge were exposed. But on the upstream side the water was deep. Gazing at the eddies and whirlpools foaming and lashing below the ledge, he recalled the ride he took across with the river high, and hoped he'd never be forced into a repeat performance; was just a mite hard on the nerves.

For some time he continued to study the formation, memorizing salient features he would discuss with Clark. Certain things the knowledge of which might prove useful to the engineer when he started making his arrangements to draw off the impounded water. The next day he'd ride down to the irrigation site for a talk. Too late to do so today . . . less than an hour till sunset. And Clark might show up in town in the course of the evening.

With a final look around, he returned to the sheriff's office.

"Glad you came back," Medford greeted him. "I found something we overlooked. May mean something to you; sure doesn't mean anything to me." He handed the Ranger a folded slip of paper.

"Was tucked under the hellion's belt," he continued. "When I moved the body for the undertaker, a corner perked out."

Unfolding the paper, Slade gazed at it, his brows drawing together.

"It's a very neatly drawn plat — the sort an engineer would draw — of some section," he said. "See, here is a trail. With a fork marked by a tiny cross. With hills on the right; one, taller than the rest, with what appears to be a double crest. Something like the Mule Ears Peaks down in the Big Bend country. I'd say that the trail before and beyond the forks runs north and south."

"But what the devil does it mean?" demanded Medford.

"Your guess is as good as mine, but I'm willing to wager it means something definite, with that drygulcher packing it," Slade answered.

"The darn thing has sort of a familiar look, but I can't place it. The section it shows, I mean. Seems to me I've seen it, but where, I got no notion," the sheriff grumbled. "Blast it! I hate puzzles."

"Sometimes they're interesting, though," Slade smiled. "This one is, decidedly. I've a feeling that if we can figure it out, it will have an important bearing on something that's going on or will be going on hereabouts."

They puzzled over the thing for some time, but could arrive at no satisfactory conclusion. Finally Slade refolded the slip and stowed it in a pocket.

"I'll hang onto it and study it some more," he said. "Well, I'm going to mosey down to Miguel's place for a while. If Clark should happen to drop into the Montezuma while you're there, tell him where I'll be and that

I want to see him."

"Okay, I will," Medford promised. "See you later."

Slade was still puzzling over the cryptic "map" when he reached the cantina. Marie was on the dance floor, so he sat down at the little table Miguel always reserved for them and spread the slip of paper on the top, knitting his brows over it. He was thus engaged when Marie joined him.

And it was Marie who gave him a clue to the thing, at least pin-pointing the location.

"What you got, Walt?" she asked. He passed the paper to her. She bent over it, her brows wrinkling slightly. Suddenly she dabbed a pink forefinger on the depicted double-crested hill.

"I know that," she said. "That's Twin Peaks. My father pointed it out to me one day when we were riding north on the trail to Espantosa Lake. The top of the hill looks like it was cut by the slice of a great big sword."

Slade nodded, and peered at the plat. "Sort of reminds me of the Tucumcari Mountains up north in New Mexico. Only their crests are rounded and look exactly like the breasts of a sleeping woman. These look to be sharp."

"They are sharp," she replied. "And

jagged; naked stone. But what does it mean, dear?"

"I'm darned if I know," Slade admitted, "but I've a hunch it was directions to that horned toad how to get somewhere, given him by somebody."

"And *I* have a hunch that whatever it is, it'll mean trouble," Marie declared. "I suppose you'll go gallivanting up there."

"Not unless I have some more definite reason for doing so," Slade answered. "Would be too much in the nature of a wild-goose chase."

Ernest Clark did not put in an appearance, so slightly after noon the following day, Slade rode down to the irrigation project for a conflab with the engineer. When he arrived there, he did not see Clark anywhere, nor did he see Amos Rolf. So he contacted one of the foremen, who appeared to be in an irritated frame of mind.

"No, I haven't got any notion where he is," said the foreman. "And he's holding up my work. I can't imagine why he isn't around. Gave me explicit instructions yesterday evening not to make a move until he gave me certain directions. Said he'd see me first thing this morning. I waited for quite a while, then knocked on the door of the shack where he sleeps, a little the other side of the main camp. Didn't get any answer. Waited some more and knocked again. Still no answer. He sure wasn't in the shack."

Slade thought a moment. "Suppose we have a look inside the shack," he suggested.

"Guess we could do worse," agreed the foreman. "He won't mind you disturbing him, if he is in there, which I'll bet a hatful of pesos he ain't. Let's go!"

He led the way to the shack in question. Slade knocked once, got no answer and turned the door knob. The door swung back easily to reveal an empty room. Over to one side was a neatly made bunk, the covers smoothed.

"Darn thing doesn't look like it's been slept in, does it?" said the foreman. "The yard man always makes it after Mr. Clark gets up. He wouldn't go in till he saw Mr. Clark was up and around."

"I'm very much of the opinion it wasn't slept in last night," Slade said. "Where does Mr. Rolf sleep?"

"In the shack over to the left," replied the foreman.

"Let's see if by any chance we can root him out," Slade suggested.

Knocking on the door of the shack brought no response. They opened the door and looked in. An empty room and another made bunk greeted their eyes.

"And that one ain't been slept in either," declared the foreman. "Maybe they went to town last night and got drunk."

"Clark was not in town last night, that I know," Slade answered.

"Well, one thing's sure for certain, he ain't here," growled the foreman. "Leaving? Okay, if Mr. Clark shows up I'll tell him you want to see him."

Slade rode back to Laredo. As he rode, he debated if he should stop for a word with Sheriff Medford, and decided against it. Turning into the trail that led to distant Espantosa Lake, he rode north at a fast pace.

"Horse," he said, "I'm playing another hunch. If it's a straight one, I only hope I'm not too late."

20

Shadow, knowing well there was something serious in the wind, quickened his gait without being told to do so.

Slade rode watchful and alert, but the trail was little travelled and he saw no one. They covered the twenty miles of which Marie had spoken in record time and the sun was still well up in the sky when Slade sighted the hill known as Twin Peaks looming above its fellows. Its naked rocks, glittering in the sunshine, gave an austere and grim, almost sinister impression. As if it had been things not good to look upon. Which was very likely the case.

When they reached the point where the trail forked, the right-hand fork, as Slade expected it would, proved to be an old Indian track winding between brush grown slopes. It was narrow, for the slopes shouldered close to its sometimes grass grown surface.

Dismounting, Slade studied the ground.

"Shadow," he said, "horses have gone in here recently, I'd say no longer ago than last night. Looks like my hunch is a straight one, all right. Okay, take it easy now. No telling what we're liable to run into on this snake track. Let's go!"

Now Slade redoubled his caution, for there were places he could not see a dozen yards ahead. He peered and listened, took careful note of every movement of birds on the wing, harkened to their calls. And constantly he scanned the sky for that indubitable proof of human presence . . . smoke.

"Some sort of a hole-up in here," he told Shadow. "These hills are dotted with old shacks and cabins built by hunters of prospectors. I'll wager one such will prove to be what we're looking for. And we don't want to come upon it all of a sudden; results might not be pleasant. So take it easy, and no noise."

Shadow jerked his head in seeming agreement, and refrained from snorting.

But the trail wound peacefully on through the slowly deepening shadows, for the slopes shut out most of the sunlight, although the sky above was still bright. With no sign of life other than that of the critters that belonged to the wastelands. Slade began to wonder if he were going to have to cross Texas to achieve his objective.

He was encouraged, however, by several times spotting fairly fresh hoof prints where the ground was soft. Once he dismounted at a point where the prints were unusually plain and studied them carefully.

"Three critters came in and one came out," he said to his mount. "Now I wonder just what that means. Be nice if we find ourselves caught between a cross-fire."

He remounted and rode on, his vigilance increasing.

And then he abruptly, on rounding a bend, sighted what he had hoped for — a thin bluish streamer mounting steadily against the brightness of the sky, which was beginning to glow with the colors of sunset.

"Smoke!" he exclaimed exultantly. "And looks to be not more than a mile ahead. Yes, horse, a straight hunch. Now if I'm just not too late. Somehow, that single horse going out makes me think I'm in time. I figure one hellion went to fetch somebody. Easy now, easy!"

A slight breeze was soughing down the depression through which the trail ran. A little later, borne on its wings, came the fragrant tang of burning wood.

"Getting close," Slade murmured to the horse. "At the first likely looking spot I'll be leaving you to take it easy for a while. Can't take a chance on your clumping much longer."

A little farther on he reached a place where the growth thinned quite a bit. Turning Shadow, he forced his way through the chaparral to where grass grew in a little clearing. He flipped out the bit and loosened the cinches, leaving the horse to graze, knowing he would not stray. Bestowing a pat on the glossy neck, he returned to the trail and eased forward on foot, slowly and cautiously, for now the smell of wood smoke was strong, mingled with it the aroma of frying meat and boiling coffee. Somebody was evidently preparing a meal, which might work to his advantage.

The adventure was nothing new to Walt Slade. Quite a few times in the course of his Ranger career he had tracked owlhoots of wideloopers to hidden hole-ups, usually some old, forgotten cabin from which they could stage their raids or lie low till things cooled down. He knew fairly well what to expect.

So he was not at all surprised when the growth again began to thin. Leaving the trail, he entered the chaparral and wormed his way through it. Behind a final fringe of leaves and branches he halted.

Set in a clearing was an old cabin. A spiral of smoke rose from its stick-and-mud chimney. The door was closed, but a light glowed behind the dirty window panes. Slade noted that the rear of the shack was close to the wall of growth. Under a leanto a couple of horses munched oats. No sound came from the cabin save an occasional faint tinny rattle, as of a cup being moved about.

Studying the clearing, he saw that a trickle of water flowed across it, doubtless bubbling from some spring in the growth. Over to one side a yawning hole with a heap of tailings beside it explained the shack's existence in this out-of-the-way place; built by a prospector who discovered metal of some sort in paying quantities. The trail ran into the clearing, crossed it and continued in a northerly direction.

Again Slade surveyed the cabin. Then, with the greatest caution, he made his way through the brush until he was behind it. As he expected, there was a rear door, also closed. Close to it was a second dirty-paned window through which light glowed.

He debated whether he should risk a look through the window, decided he would. Now it was almost full dark and he did not think he would be detected by anybody inside; and it would be greatly to his advantage to learn the layout of the shack before attempting to crash the rear door. He dared not risk lifting the latch, for the door might be bolted on the inside. Gliding forward, he reached the window, peered through.

The single room was rudely furnished with a home-made table and chairs. There was a stone fireplace, glowing with coals. Several bunks were built along the walls, a couple of them quite new. On shelves were staple provisions. Cooking utensils were scattered about.

Seated at the table, were two men. The one facing Slade, the Ranger did not recollect ever seeing. He had a hard-lined countenance and was eating greedily.

Seated across the table from him, securely bound to a chair, head bowed over his untouched plate, his whole attitude expressive of dejection and despair, was Ernest Clark.

After the one quick glance, Slade eased back to the brush, exactly back of the closed door. He took a deep breath, bounded forward and hit the door with his shoulder, all his two hundred pounds of bone and muscle behind it.

The door slammed open with a bang, and

Slade was in the room. The man on the far side of the table stared with bulging eyes, paralyzed into inaction by the unexpected suddenness of the assault. And that instant of hesitation was fatal. He went for his gun, but before he could reach it, the barrel of Slade's Colt crashed against his skull and dropped him senseless to the floor. Slade rounded the table, plucked the gun from its sheath and tossed it aside.

Ernest Clark gave a croaking cry of joy. "Slade!" he panted. "Where — how —"

"Hold the questions till later," Slade snapped. "I've got things to do. Kneeling, he went to work on the cords that bound Clark to the chair. His steely fingers quickly loosened the knots. He did not cut the lashes, having use for them. Freed, Clark tried to rise, but his numbed legs refused to support him and he fell back into the chair. Slade picked him up, chair and all, and deposited him in a corner where he was out of sight from both windows.

"Rub some feeling back into your legs," he said, and turned his attention to the unconscious abductor. With the lashings, he tied hands and feet securely, stuffed a handkerchief lightly into the fellow's mouth and secured it in place with his neckerchief. Then he shoved the limp form under one of the bunks and straightened up.

"If he choked to death, it won't be much loss," he said to Clark, who was busily massaging his numbed limbs. "Now suppose you tell me what happened to you. Talk fast, we may not have much time."

"I hardly know," the engineer replied. "I stepped out of the door of my shack, figuring to go to town. Two men grabbed me. One shoved a gun into my ribs and told me to keep quiet. They led me to where horses stood, made me mount one and tied my ankles to the stirrup straps. Then, after again telling me to keep quiet if I wanted to stay alive, they mounted and we rode, it seemed to me all night. They brought me to this place and tied me to the chair. Why they didn't kill me at once, I don't know, for I gathered from their conversation they didn't intend I should leave this cabin alive. One said he was going to tell the Boss they had me and to come ahead. I heard him ride away. The other remained here, all day. Why didn't they kill me at once?"

"Because," Slade replied quietly, "you have some information or something somebody desires. When the Boss got here, they would have *persuaded* you to talk before they murdered you."

"But in heaven's name who is the Boss?"

Clark asked.

"Your *amigo,* Amos Rolf," Slade answered.

Clark's jaw sagged; his eyes seemed likely to drop out of his head.

"Slade!" he stuttered, "That — that is incredible."

"Perhaps, but you'll find out before the evening is over.

"That is," he added grimly, "if we both manage to stay alive."

As he spoke, he drew something from a cunningly concealed secret pocket in his broad leather belt and pinned it to his shirt front, a gleaming silver star set on a silver circle, the feared and honored badge of the Texas Rangers. The time for cover-up was past.

Wordless, Clark stared at the symbol of law and order and justice for all. Finally he spoke, slowly, "So that's what you are. Well, I should have guessed it. You are just what I've always heard the Rangers to be. And I guess you know what you're talking about."

"I do," Slade answered. "Will explain everything later."

Closing the back door, he jammed a chair under the knob. He carried another chair to a corner, from which he had a view of the front door, and sat down.

"Now all we can do is wait," he said. "Stay

right where you are, no matter what happens. Know how to handle a gun?" The engineer shook his head.

"Then you're better off without one," Slade said. "Okay, just stay put. No more talking, now."

The wait was tedious, but it proved to be not very long. Little more than half an hour had elapsed when Slade's ears caught the soft clump of horses' hoofs entering the clearing, then the sound of voices. He stood up, moved forward a couple of steps. There was a jingle of bridle irons, a pause. Then two men opened the front door and entered, blinking at the light.

Slightly to the front was a squat individual with squinted eyes. The other was Amos Rolf.

Slade's voice rang out, "In the name of the State of Texas! You are under arrest! Elevate!"

There was an instant of utter amazement, then the squat man let out a yelp,

"The hellion's a Ranger!"

"Get him!" roared Rolf. His right hand whipped across to his left armpit. The squat man also went for his gun.

Slade drew and shot. The squat man fell without a groan, a blue hole between his squinty eyes. Slade whipped aside as Rolf fired, and the bullet missed its mark. He shot again, to wound, not to kill, for he earnestly desired to take Rolf alive.

But he had underestimated Rolf's tremendous vitality. The slug went home, causing Rolf to drop his gun, but he only grunted, bounded forward into the blaze of Slade's Colt, slammed it from his grip and closed, both his huge hands gripping *El Halcón*'s throat. Slade seized his wrists and managed to loosen the hold a little, but could not break it. He dared not let go to reach for his other gun, for he instinctively knew the full grip of those mighty hands would snap his neck like a reed.

Rolf was a big man, pounds heavier than the tall Ranger, and despite his wound, his strength was that of a maniac. Slade tore at his wrists, but break that awful hold he could not. Red flashes were storming before his eyes, bells rang in his ears. Another moment and his strength would begin to ebb from sheer suffocation. Rolf's rage-contorted face was close to his, eyes gleaming in triumph.

His senses whirling, Slade remembered a trick he had used in a hand-to-hand struggle once before. With a last supreme effort, he hurled himself backward and down, gripping Rolf's wrist and jerking down with all his remaining strength. At the same time his leg drove upward, rigid as a bar of steel, his foot catching Rolf squarely in the midriff. He jerked again, and let go the wrists.

Rolf's body hurtled through the air as if he had taken unto himself wings. His head struck the stone fireplace with a sodden crunch and he fell to the floor, to lie motionless. Slade struggled to his feet, gun ready. It was not needed.

Clark was white to the lips, his eyes wide and horror-filled.

"God in Heaven!" he choked. "Smashed his skull like an egg shell! His brains are oozing out!"

"Yes," Slade panted wearily. "Brains that guided into the right channels would have taken him far. But brains prostituted to evil!" He righted an overturned chair, sat down and with fingers that shook a little rolled a cigarette.

"You all right?" Clark asked anxiously.

"My neck's sore as the devil, but otherwise I'm okay," Slade replied. "Blazes, what a pair of hands! I never felt their equal."

After a couple of deep drags, he unpinned the Ranger star and returned it to its hiding place.

"Forget you ever saw it," he told Clark. "Looks like I'm still under cover hereabouts,

I hope."

"I will," the engineer promised, understanding perfectly. "Now what?"

"As soon as I finish my smoke, I'll drag the carcasses to one side and then go look after my horse and the other critters."

"And while you're at it, I'll try and fix us something to eat," Clark said. "Coffee still steaming in the pot and there's plenty of food on the shelves. I'll get the fire going right away. I imagine you can stand a bite, and so can I. Didn't have much appetite before," he concluded with a wan smile.

"I imagine you didn't," Slade agreed. "Okay, that'll be fine. We're in no hurry. I want that gentleman under the bunk to get his senses back before we move on. He isn't hurt much, and I expect he'll be able to tie up a few loose ends for us when he's in condition to talk."

After getting the bodies out of the way, Slade went outside and whistled a loud note. A few minutes and Shadow came trotting across the clearing, snorting inquiringly. Slade removed the rig and poured a helping of oats into a feed box. Unsaddling the horses Rolf and his companion had ridden, he treated them to some provender.

Returning to the cabin, he found Clark, who was not a bad cook, had a meal well under way. Before long they sat down to the food and hot coffee both sorely needed.

They had finished their surrounding and were smoking when the man under the bunk began to groan and mutter with returning consciousness. Slade hauled him out, untied him and removed the gag. A few more minutes and he opened his eyes and stared dazedly. Slade lifted him and deposited him in a chair. He apparently had fully recovered his faculties.

Slade sat down opposite him and regarded him steadily for perhaps half a minute. The fellow blanched and cringed, completely cowed by that bleak stare.

"Ready to talk, and stay alive?" Slade asked.

"I'll talk," the man mouthed thickly. "What do you want me to say?"

"Why did Rolf have Mr. Clark kidnapped, what did he want of him?"

"He wanted him to write a letter to the president of the company, telling him he was quitting, and leaving for a job way down in Mexico," the other replied. "To tell him Rolf would take over everything till somebody else was sent out. The president believed in Rolf and he would have managed to stay in charge long enough to mess things up, after he'd gotten rid of you, which he figured to do. Reckon that's where he made a mistake."

"Looks sort of that way," Slade nodded. "And was Rolf backed by the Neches Waterway people?"

"Really I don't know," the man answered. "If he was he never said so. Never said much of anything about himself, but he paid well." Slade believed the fellow was telling the truth.

"That's what I was afraid of," he remarked to Clark. "That's why I was so anxious to take Rolf alive, if possible. As it is, we have nothing definite against the instigators of the whole rotten business. Well, they'll travel their road to the end appointed."

"And I've a notion it won't be a nice end," Clark commented dryly, after a look at Slade's face. "Reckon they're sort of in the nature of unfinished business for you."

"In a way," Slade admitted. He turned to the prisoner again.

"Talk freely to the sheriff and perhaps things will be easier," he said. "I'll say a word for you if you do. If you don't, with the charges that can be put against you, you'll stay in jail till you trip over your whiskers. Now I'll take care of that cut on your head."

With medicants from his saddle pouches

he cleaned, treated and bandaged the wound.

"Feller," the prisoner mumbled when he had finished, "that feels a devil of a sight better. You ain't so bad."

"I try not to be, so long as folks don't force me to be otherwise," Slade returned.

"Like Rolf did," the other nodded. "Well, he found out it didn't pay. Guess he had it coming. And you cleaned up the last of our bunch tonight."

Turning to Clark, Slade said, "Give him some coffee and then go out and saddle those two horses under the leanto; they're fresh. The moon will be up soon and we'll be going. Sheriff Medford can pick up the bodies tomorrow."

As they mounted for the trip to town, Slade said to the prisoner, "I'm not going to make you uncomfortable by tying your ankles to the straps, but you'll ride a little ahead of us, and don't forget, this saddle gun of mine carries a long ways."

"Think I'm a plumb darn fool?" the prisoner replied in an injured voice. "After what you promised me, I'd ride to town alone, give myself up and get it over with." He raised his head, squared his shoulders. Slade believed he was a man who henceforth would ride the straight trail. He resolved to

235

have a talk with Judge Arbaugh before leaving Laredo.

As a matter of fact, some years later Walt Slade would shake hands with a certain hard-faced rancher who had managed to save enough money to buy a small spread and was doing all right by himself.

The ride to Laredo was without incident. The prisoner was turned over to the sheriff and after giving him an account of what happened, Slade and Clark called it a night.

Medford brought in the bodies the following day and an inquest was held. Clark's evidence, backed up by what the prisoner had to say, was conclusive and a verdict of justifiable homicide was quickly returned.

"Well, that takes care of that," Slade said to the sheriff. "Now they can go ahead and turn your valley into a garden spot without further hindrance."

Medford nodded agreement.

"Tell McNelty hello for me, and old man Dunn, too, when you see him," he said. "Guess you're on your way."

"Yes, the chances are Captain Jim will have another chore lined up for me by the time I get back to the Post," Slade replied.

It was Marie who watched him ride away, tall and graceful atop his great black horse, to where duty called and danger and new adventure waited.

And they did not say goodbye when they parted, but "*hasta luego* . . . till we meet again!"

DATE DUE

FEB 2 2 2012	JAN 3 0 2019
APR 1 1 2012	MAR 2 8 2019
AUG 2 1 2012	
SEP 7 2012	
OCT 1 7 2012	
MAY 0 7 2013	
NOV 0 1 2013	
JAN 2 9 2016	
AUG 1 6 2016	
SEP 2 0 2016	
NOV 1 9 2018	